I0592840

Originally published as *Bright and Yellow, Hard and Cold*

A TRACE OF GOLD
MURDER CHICAGO STYLE

TIM CHAPMAN

Author of

The Blue Silence

Kiddieland and other misfortunes

Thrilling Tales
Chicago, IL

Thrilling Tales
Chicago, IL

www.thrillingtales.com

This is a work of fiction. Descriptions and portrayals of real
people, events, organizations, or establishments are intended
to provide background for the story and are used fictitiously.
Other characters and situations are drawn from the author's
imagination and are not intended to be real.

Book and cover design by Tim Chapman

ISBN: 978-0-9862862-0-9

Library of Congress Control Number: 2014921056

Acknowledgments

My thanks to Tara Ison and Sandi Wisenberg for getting me started; to Linda Landrigan for her encouragement; to Emily Victorson for her input; to writers Libby Fischer Hellmann, Sara Paretsky, Irene Westcott, Sherry Thomas, Kayte Korwitts, Lisa Grayson, Molly Dumbleton, Mike Smith, Jeff Cockrell, and Joseph Theroux for their feedback; to the FBI for their public database; and to my wife and muse, Ellen, for keeping me honest—take a bow, sugarbeet!

Gold! gold! gold! gold!
Bright and yellow, hard and cold,
Molten, graven, hammered and rolled,
Heavy to get, and light to hold,
Hoarded, bartered, bought and sold,
Stolen, borrowed, squandered, doled,
Spurned by the young, but hugged by the old
To the verge of the churchyard mould;
Price of many a crime untold.
Gold! gold! gold! gold!
Good or bad a thousand-fold!
How widely its agencies vary—
To save—to ruin—to curse—to bless

—Thomas Hood

A TRACE OF GOLD

He would never have guessed that a man in his eighties could hold out that long. He had beaten the old guy senseless and revived him three times and he finally had to concede that he didn't know any more than when he started, which was squat. He hadn't been sure he could torture an old man, let alone kill one. The old guy's stooped frame and white hair kind of reminded him of his grandfather, or at least what he imagined his grandfather would have been like had he known him. Anyway, it was too late for second thoughts. It was stiflingly hot in the house and hard to breathe with all the dog hair floating around, so he'd taken off his mask. The old guy'd be able to identify him now and he knew he couldn't make a deal with him. Not after killing his dogs. If anything could have made him talk it would have been that. The man wailed through the tape over his mouth when he shot them. In a way he'd be better off dead. If he left him alive the old guy would spend the rest of his life grieving over a couple of mutts.

The old man was still unconscious, which made it easier. He walked around behind him, pressed the little automatic against the back of his head and pulled the trigger, twice. The man jerked a little and slumped forward, straining the extension cord that held him to the kitchen chair. He wasn't sure whether he'd be able to feel a pulse through the latex gloves he wore, so he put his ear next to the man's open mouth and listened for breathing. He was startled by a low, raspy sound as the old man's weight against the cord forced air from his lungs.

He took his beer with him into the bathroom and set it on the back of the toilet while he pissed. He'd brought a duffel bag

---

filled with supplies and he wanted to make certain he didn't leave anything behind, especially a beer can with his DNA on it. He swore when the latex gloves made it hard to zip up his pants. After flushing the toilet twice he went back to the kitchen. He tossed the beer can and gun into his bag. The last thing he did was cut the extension cord that held the old man in his seat. Gravity slowly pulled the body out of the chair. The old man rolled onto his back and stopped, staring up at him from the green and white tiles. He turned the head to one side with his foot while he coiled the cord and tossed it into his bag. That way the old guy could look at his dogs until someone found them. The blood stood out dark on the linoleum, and he avoided the puddles as he stepped over the body. He checked to see that the back door was locked before walking down the steps, out the gate, and into the night.

ONE

It was a muggy day and Sean McKinney was conscious of the perspiration on his back as he walked up the steps of the criminal courts building at 26th and California Streets on Chicago's near south side. He had rehearsed his speech several times in the car on the short drive from the crime lab, but his stomach still tightened as he entered Courtroom 207. The courtroom was a monument to tradition in oak and stone and it smelled musty, with a hint of disinfectant. The smell of law, McKinney thought. He leaned against the cool surface of a marble wall and fiddled with the wedding ring in his pocket, slipping it on and off his finger as he surveyed the room. The judge hadn't yet entered, but the attorneys were at their respective tables. McKinney wasn't quite six feet tall and thin, his unkempt, sand-colored hair and crooked nose making him look more like a middle-aged beach bum than a forensic scientist with the Illinois State Police. He wiped his palms on his chinos as he approached the state's attorney's table. Earlier that week the lead prosecutor, Brian Jameson, had let him know that McKinney's report and bench notes, detailing his examination of the evidence, were not important to the case and would not be shared with the defense.

McKinney caught a look of disdain as Jameson spotted him. Jameson was well known for his six hundred dollar suits and his no-nonsense demeanor. In the three years McKinney had known Jameson he had never seen him smile. Back at the crime lab, they joked that the guy had a notch on his briefcase for every trial he'd won.

"McKinney," Jameson said. "What are you doing here?"

"I've brought copies of my report and notes for you and the defense," McKinney said. "Here's your copy." He held out a manila folder. When the attorney didn't take it he laid it on the table.

"I told you last week," Jameson said, "I'm not using your report. Phillips confessed and your examination of the hair evidence doesn't impact our case."

"It doesn't *help* your case, you mean." He pointed to the manila folder. "I found dog hair all over the victim's clothing but there wasn't one dog hair on Phillips's clothes. The killer wrestled with old Mr. Drenon. He touched his clothes. He probably sat on his furniture. Some dog hair would likely have been transferred to the killer's clothing."

"Absence of evidence isn't evidence of absence, McKinney. You know that."

"That's true, and it's up to you to make that case to the jury, but they deserve to hear all the relevant facts. Don't you have a duty to turn my findings over to the defense as part of discovery?"

"Not if we don't use your report in preparing our case. You couldn't get a match, so we're not using your report. End of discussion."

"Be reasonable, Jameson. Why doesn't any of the physical evidence point to this guy? There was blood all over the kitchen but not one drop was found on your suspect. There was a partial footprint on the victim's cheek but it doesn't match any of the suspect's shoes. Arnold Drenon and his dogs were shot, but there was no gunshot residue on Phillips's hands. The medical examiner estimates the time of death right before he was picked up. When did he have time to change his clothes and clean up?"

Jameson glared at McKinney. His voice, when he spoke, was low and tightly controlled. "He confessed. We have a confession."

"See, that's what I don't understand. He's obviously pleading not guilty or you wouldn't be here today. So, why did he confess?" McKinney's blue eyes bored into Jameson, trying to read the other man. There were plenty of reasons why someone would confess to a murder he didn't commit. Maybe the police were a little overzealous in the interrogation room. Maybe the guy was one of those publicity-hungry nutcases, the kind that think lonely women will write to them in prison. McKinney looked across to the defense table. The twenty-something-year-old man sitting there rocked slowly back and forth while his eyes darted around the courtroom. His movements made McKinney think of a cornered cat. He looked back at Jameson.

Jameson glanced away.

"Is he mentally challenged in some way? What was his motive? The cops don't think it was burglary. There was plenty of money and jewelry still in the house."

"I don't know, maybe he doesn't like dogs. Go back to the lab, McKinney. You're not a lawyer and you're not a cop. You look at little bits of garbage under a microscope all day and that's where your job ends. Get out of here before I call Director Roberts and flush your career down the toilet."

McKinney smiled. "Did you know that some species of aphid are able to reproduce without the benefit of a mate? It's called parthenogenesis."

"So what?" Jameson asked.

"I suggest you try it."

McKinney turned and walked over to the defense table. The defense, he knew, consisted of one woman—a tired public defender, Nina Anderson—who was overworked, underpaid and had stopped caring about her clients after she managed to get a rapist's case thrown out on a technicality. Two weeks later, the same man raped and killed a ten-year-old girl. McKinney had seen her in court since then and it seemed as though she was just going through the motions.

Seated next to Anderson was a pasty-faced young man in a suit two sizes too small. Watching John Phillips rock back and forth, McKinney had the vague impression that he knew the man from somewhere. He didn't look like the sort of person who would torture and kill a little old man. McKinney sighed. One thing he had learned long ago was that anyone is capable of anything. You couldn't tell whether a person was guilty or innocent of a crime by looking at them, talking to them, or even hearing a confession or eyewitness account of the crime. The only thing that never lies is the physical evidence, and that requires skill to interpret. A skill he had spent years honing.

Counselor Anderson looked up from her notes. Her messy blonde hair was shot through with streaks of gray and her fingernails had been chewed down to the quick. Despite her disheveled appearance, McKinney thought she was an attractive woman. He wondered what she looked like when she smiled.

"May I help you?" she asked.

McKinney looked at the manila folder in his hand. The hand shook a little. He sighed and dropped the folder on the table in front of her. As he walked out of the courtroom he looked at the state's attorney's table. Jameson was making a flushing motion with his hand. He mouthed the word, "whoosh."

It was too late in the day to go back to the lab, so McKinney decided to head home. He slipped a Magic Sam CD into the player on the dash and drove north along the lake, his windows open to let in the fresh, cool smell of the lake air. He went over the case in his mind. He was convinced that Jameson didn't have enough evidence to bring the kid to trial, but he wasn't certain that circumventing the state's attorney had been the right thing to do. It was bound to get him in trouble.

When he got home to his Wrigleyville apartment he found his daughter, Angelina, sitting on the back steps leading to their third floor walk-up, reading a book. Living in Wrigleyville had been his idea—easy access to Cubs games and less expensive than the Lincoln Park condo they had lived in when his wife was alive. As a kid, he had spent so many summer days sitting in the Wrigley Field bleachers that his parents teased him they could see ivy growing on his legs. Now, going to a game held no interest for him. McKinney looked up at Angelina as he trudged up the steps. The setting sun bathed her in a warm, summery glow.

"Ciao, Bella. How was summer school?"

"Hey, Dad. School was fine." She held up her book for him to see, a collection of short stories by Flannery O'Connor. "Homework. Oh...and Director Roberts called. He wants you to call him back."

He grimaced. "Ugh."

"Rough day at work?"

McKinney kicked some dirt off the wooden step below her and plopped himself down. This was his favorite part of the day, coming home to spend time with his daughter, and he sat smiling up at her. Angelina's mother, Catherine, was an Italian beauty who had died after a prolonged battle with breast cancer. McKinney had barely held on to his job after that. He became moody and withdrawn, spending most of his time sitting alone in his study, not really doing anything, just staring. Slowly, he became aware that having a teenage daughter who had lost her mother was a responsibility that wouldn't allow him to indulge his grief. Still, Angelina had taken over the job of piloting the family finances. She balanced the checkbook, made certain the bills were paid, and came up with a budget that McKinney had a hard time sticking to. She had inherited her mother's resourcefulness, along with her long, dark hair and olive skin, but at sixteen was still a little gangly. McKinney was gangly at fifty. He hoped Angelina wasn't wading in that part of his family's gene pool. McKinney called her Bella because, on the day she was born, he knew that she was the most beautiful thing he had ever seen or would ever see again. On her thirteenth birthday she declared that she was no longer a little girl and asked McKinney to call her by her given name. He tried, but it was a tough habit to break. Looking up at her now he felt that same amalgam of pride and wonder that he was sure no other parent could know.

"I gave one of my reports to the public defender without having been subpoenaed or getting permission from the state's attorney. I think her client is being set up to take the rap for something he didn't do. Director Roberts and most of the folks at the lab act like we're an arm of the State's Attorney's Office. They don't understand how much forensic science depends on objectivity. I'm worried about repercussions, though. It would be nice if I could afford to send you to college in a couple of years."

"Well, Director Roberts sounded pretty mad."

"Roberts," McKinney snorted. "All he cares about is avoiding controversy until he can retire and collect his pension." He hooked a hand over the banister and pulled himself to his feet. "I'll call the lab now and smooth things over." He kissed her on her furrowed teenaged brow as he sidled past her on the steps. "Did you feed and walk Hendrix yet?

"Not yet," she said. "I've been studying."

"Well, let's get going," he said. "I don't want us to be late for tai chi class." As he opened the screen door and stepped into their kitchen a big, black poodle launched his furry, wagging fifty pounds at McKinney's stomach.

TWO

The woods in Rockcastle County, Kentucky were aflame with the color of the blossoming redbuds in the spring of 1933, and Delroy was burning up. He finished buckling rough-hewn, leather straps to the mule and looked out at the barren fields. As a child Delroy had loved to run through the hills, eating wild blackberries in the woods and sunning himself on the big, flat rock that jutted out from the cliffs behind the farm. He had loved the land, but now his morning coffee and biscuits turned to acid in his stomach at the thought of toiling over the dry, cracked field.

Delroy's daddy had died in a muddy trench in the Ardennes. His older brothers, Pike and Joe, worked the farm after that, but times were tough and what they got from the landowner wasn't enough to sustain a family. Finally, they sent Momma to live with her sister in Stony Point. Not too long after, the two older boys packed up and went to California. They, like thousands of others, had gone west looking for decent jobs but, from their letters, it was obvious that they were working as fruit tramps, living in tent cities, and breaking their backs for a few cents a day. Despite the sorry reports from his brothers, Delroy wanted off the farm, too. The redbuds blooming in the surrounding hills mocked him with their intensity as he followed the plow up and down the rows of freshly turned earth. They reminded him of Lucille.

Lucille knew about another fire that burned in Delroy. Sometimes she'd run her long, red hair across his arm just to watch him twitch. He'd shudder and say, "By God, if you ain't the one." She might as well have touched him with a live wire.

Twice a week, when he came in from the fields, he took a stiff brush and scrubbed his hands raw in an effort to get the dirt out from under his nails before walking the three miles to Lucille's house. He wouldn't let her see him with unclean hands. He was barely out of his teens and only a year older than Lucille, but he treated her gallantly, the way he imagined his father had treated his mother before he'd gone off to get himself killed. Delroy'd slick his blond hair down with pomade and put on his good shirt and shoes, but there was no way to hide his farmer's red neck and calloused hands. Lucille's family didn't much care for Delroy. They didn't see any future for her with a tenant farmer, and her older brother especially hated him. Delroy had pounded the pudding out of Jordan once for calling his family croppers. He knew they were, but he didn't like to have it pointed out in front of everyone.

Delroy let the mule rest and crouched down in the middle of the field to examine the dirt. He picked up a clod and squeezed it, watching the meager black soil separate from the clay. It sifted through his fingers and onto the leg of his overalls. What remained in his hand was a mix of nutrient-poor clay and pebbles. Drought and heat had exhausted the earth. Root vegetables wouldn't grow in the hard clay, and the corn and beans had been a sorry lot for two years running. This year's crop would be worse. He knew he was licked. He got up, trudged back to the derelict house and went back to bed. The slats on his bedroom walls had warped enough to let in a few shafts of early morning sun. The murky light accentuated the room's emptiness. One stray beam illuminated a picture of his parents, hanging on the wall opposite the iron bed. It had been taken on their wedding day. Delroy pulled the dusty blanket over his head.

Later that day he packed a bag, took the hobbles off the mule, kicked open the gate to the feed yard, and started for Lucille's. Before he left he pried a square-headed nail out of the bottom of the door frame and thrust it into his pocket. It was one of the few his older brothers had let him hammer in when they had rebuilt the house after a fire. He had been born and raised on that farm, but he didn't look back.

He and Lucille hitched a ride to Frankfort. Delroy paid two dollars for the justice of the peace to marry them and five dollars for a hotel room to consummate the marriage. They consummated all night and all the next morning, right up until checkout time. Then he really shook the moths out of his coin purse and bought them two tickets on the Greyhound bus to Chicago. For the first time since his father died he felt free, and he was both exhilarated and frightened by it. He stayed awake through most of the trip, holding Lucille's hand and pushing his face against the window. He wanted to see everything there was to see. The bus took them through big cities and small towns as it wound its way north and Delroy jumped off at every rest stop to look at the people and smell the air.

At night the bus rumbled along the quiet country roads and Delroy strained to see into the blackness. Even the rise and fall of the telephone wires strung alongside the road seemed exotic to him. He imagined that was what the ocean waves were like. The moonlight coming through the window made Lucille's pale skin glow, soft and blue-white. Her red hair looked darker. She was sleeping with her mouth open, and Delroy noticed a pearl of saliva on her lower lip. It seemed, somehow, precious to him. Here he was, with his wife sleeping on his shoulder and his days of scraping a living out of the barren earth behind him. *This*, he thought, *is happiness*. Lucille opened her eyes and saw Delroy smiling down at her. She leaned up and kissed him. "Country boy," she said, "you are somethin' else."

Chicago was almost too much for them—too much noise, too much traffic, and too many people. Lucille's cousin Edna had given them the name and address of a woman who'd rent them a room. She lived at 35th and Lake Park Avenue. Edna said they were lucky to get it because, in a few months, the neighborhood would be swarming with people from all over the country going to the World's Fair. It took them a while to get directions and, when they did, it was over thirty blocks from the bus station. They walked the whole way to save money. Tired as he was, Delroy drank in the city with an unquenchable thirst—car exhaust, over-ripe fruit, honking, screaming, laughing, gray suits, blue dresses, hats with yellow feathers, tall, brick buildings. Every few blocks they'd stop and Delroy would marvel as he wiped the sweat off his face and switched the big suitcase that contained all of their possessions from one hand to the other. They floated through the throngs on the sidewalk like people walking in a dream. They didn't notice the two men who had followed them from the depot until it was too late. The short, burly one slammed into Delroy's shoulder, knocking him off balance and into Lucille. Delroy shouted, "Hey!" and set down the suitcase as the man ran off. That was the cue for the second man, who slid in between them, picked up the case, and ran in the opposite direction. Delroy took off after him but the man moved smoothly, weaving in and out of the crowd on the sidewalk. Delroy chased him for a few blocks, but the man had got the jump on him and the same sea of humanity that opened for the thief thwarted Delroy's progress. Finally, thief and suitcase disappeared down a side street. When Delroy got back to Lucille she was sitting on the curb. At the sight of his empty hands she started crying.

"The Bible my granma gave me is in that suitcase and all our clothes and everything. Why'd you let him take that?"

Delroy felt like he'd been stabbed in the heart with an icicle. "What do you mean let him? I chased that guy for three blocks. I tried to get the suitcase back but I lost him in the crowd."

"Well, what are we gonna do?"

"Do? There's nothing to do. Some guy sees a couple of country folk and decides to help himself. I don't believe the police can do us any good, so let's just get to where we're going."

"But all my things…"

Delroy reached out his hand to help Lucille up. She looked at it for a minute, pushed herself up, and started walking off down the sidewalk. Delroy looked down at his empty hand and turned to follow her.

THREE

Gilbert Anglin considered himself to be a fastidious person. The top of his dresser was dust free and his watch, wallet, keys, and change were all neatly arranged in a little felt-lined tray. When he wasn't working he dressed his six-foot frame in Nautica and Calvin Klein. He regularly paid thirty-five bucks to have his wavy, brown hair styled. Despite this attention to detail, his square face and crooked nose made him look like a thug. Tonight he was working, and that meant cargo pants and black leather military boots. He looked around the furnished studio apartment as he dressed. It contained a scattering of used motel furniture set on an ancient shag carpet, everything clean and orderly but nondescript. The bare, pea-green walls produced an institutional atmosphere that complemented Gilbert's self-imposed seclusion. *One good score*, he thought, *and dumps like this are history.* He finished packing his pry bar and lock picks in the false bottom of his duffel bag, tossed a ball of clothesline, a box of latex gloves, and a towel on top and zipped the bag closed.

Finding the gold hidden by the Barker/Karpis gang had been a dream of his father's, but hunting down the friends and family of the gang members who buried it way back in 1935 was Gilbert's idea. He was tired of making his living burgling fat suburbanites. Sometimes, the risks outweighed the benefits. He needed a big score and he needed it soon; that old gangster gold could be that score.

In June of 1962 his father, John Anglin, his uncle Clarence, and another man crawled out of their cells at Alcatraz through holes they had cut to the utility corridor. They crawled through an air vent to the roof and kicked across the treacherous mile and a half of choppy Pacific to the mainland on an improvised raft. Their escape wasn't noticed right away because they left dummies in their bunks to fool the guards. They had fashioned the dummies' heads out of plaster of Paris, which they then painted and outfitted with hair from the prison barbershop. They got the plaster of Paris from Alvin Karpis. Karpis had been at Alcatraz since 1936. Back in the '30s he was a prominent member of the Barker/Karpis gang, along with Freddie and Doc Barker. They had terrorized the Depression-era Midwest with a series of bank robberies and kidnappings. One of the kidnappings, that of Minneapolis banker Edward Bremer, had netted them two hundred thousand dollars. According to Karpis, the money had been converted to gold coins in Cuba, brought back to the U.S., and buried. Most of the gang were captured or killed before they had a chance to recover it. Karpis managed to dodge the feds for a couple of years more, but his status as Public Enemy Number One kept him on the run. Karpis claimed that Freddie Barker and Ma, the Barker boys' mother, had hidden the gold somewhere near Lake Weir in Florida where they were killed in a gun battle with the FBI. In 1935, gold was selling for thirty-five dollars an ounce. Gilbert estimated that, at today's rates, it would be worth over four million dollars.

After the escape, Gilbert's father spent his life on the run, keeping his family moving from town to town. Gilbert couldn't recall how many last names he'd had as a child but he could count the number of friends on one hand. They hadn't been allowed to get close to anyone and his father's paranoia eventually took its toll on his mother. Two days after Gilbert's ninth birthday she took the ice bucket from the dresser of the cheap motel they were stopping at and said she was going down to the lobby for sodas. She disappeared into the hot Arizona night and he never saw her again. His father rarely spoke to him after that and, when he did, it was mostly long rambling reminiscences about his escape from Alcatraz and the convicts he'd met inside. Gilbert received little in the way of guidance from his criminal father but what he did receive added up to this—birds are meant for plucking, and someone knew where the Barkers hid a fortune in gold.

Gilbert dropped the heavy duffel bag next to the little desk in his room and took out a folder of charts and maps. He had researched everyone he could find who knew Karpis in Alcatraz and back in the 1930s. He had studied Karpis's movements after his release from prison in 1969 until his death in 1979. That gold was still out there. For some reason Karpis had never gone after it. Gilbert had compiled this information from his father's ramblings, Internet searches, personal interviews, and FBI files. He charted everyone's movements by time and locale and eventually realized that almost all of the gang members who had anything to do with Karpis were dead. If they hadn't been gunned down by G-men they had succumbed to disease or old age. Famous thieves like John Dillinger and Pretty Boy Floyd were now just a colorful part of American history, and second-tier hoods like Shotgun George Zeigler and Volney Davis were obscure footnotes in a handful of true crime books. Some of the men had wives or girlfriends though, and a few of these women were still alive.

Gilbert knew that, when it came to getting their dicks massaged, men were stupid. They bragged about their exploits when they were trying to impress some broad and, afterwards, when they were relaxed and sleepy, they talked about the big plans they had for the future. One of these women must have heard something that could help him find the gold.

Gilbert had hoped to get a line on Wynona Burdett, the girlfriend of gang member Harry Campbell. Harry and Wynona had been in Florida with Karpis in January of '35. They had been fishing at Little River and were going to drive back up the coast to the Barkers' place on Lake Weir when they were tipped off that Ma and Freddie had been killed in a shoot-out with the feds. Harry Campbell died in prison, and Wynona died in a nursing home. However, Wynona's younger sister, Florence, was living in the Chicago suburb of Bensenville. Bensenville was where the Barker/Karpis gang had kept a hideout during the '30s. This coincidence wasn't lost on Gilbert. He was optimistic as he jotted down the address and slid his files back in the desk drawer. He checked the action on his little Beretta .25 automatic and slipped it into his front pants pocket.

"Thank God for little sisters," he said.

He was whistling as he walked out the door.

FOUR

McKinney sat at a desk covered with Lucite-encased insects, reference manuals, empty coffee cups, and a photograph of his family he had taken years before at the Lincoln Park Zoo. In it, Catherine held a sleeping baby Angelina while, in the background, a mother ape held her own baby.

It was mid-afternoon and he had just finished writing a report on a gunshot residue case when his telephone rang. The case had come into the lab the night before, but it was high priority and his supervisor asked him to work it right away. A child had been killed in a drive-by shooting and the cops had a suspect in custody. The media was all over it.

McKinney had analyzed the samples the police collected from the suspect's hands and shirtsleeves when he was arrested. He used a scanning electron microscope with an electron beam exciter and X-ray detector to search each sample for unique particles containing the right combination of barium, lead, and antimony. The instrument ran all night long, scanning the four samples. It found nothing.

Some gangbangers knew that gunshot residue was blown back onto their hands when they fired a gun, so they would hurry to wash it off before the police picked them up. Some had even been caught in alleys, urinating on their hands in an attempt to wash away the evidence. Either this suspect hadn't fired the gun or he had washed his hands before he was arrested. Whatever the case, McKinney couldn't put a gun in his hand and he was disappointed. He hoped the ringing phone wasn't a reporter. He reached through the stacks of papers on his desk and, reluctantly, picked it up.

"McKinney here."

"Mr. McKinney, this is Nina Anderson, the public defender for John Phillips. I was wondering if we could get together and talk about his case."

Crap, McKinney thought. He didn't regret giving her his report but it had taken him over an hour to mollify Director Roberts. "What would you like to know, Ms. Anderson?"

There was a pause before she spoke. "I think I understand your work on the evidence from your notes. What I would like is your advice. Couldn't we do this informally, perhaps over lunch?"

McKinney was caught off guard. Defense attorneys didn't call the lab very often and, when they did, it was usually to make sure he'd received a subpoena or to schedule a deposition. The defense generally considered forensic scientists part of the opposing team. They certainly never asked for advice. "We have a conference room here at the lab," he said, stiffly. "We can talk there if you'd like."

"I appreciate the assistance you've given me already, Mr. McKinney. Knowing Brian Jameson, I imagine you took some heat for it. I just thought it would be easier for you if you weren't seen meeting with the enemy."

McKinney fiddled with the encapsulated corpse of a wasp beetle while he talked. Some of his fellow scientists didn't like or trust defense attorneys. Most of the time they testified in court on behalf of the prosecution. It was the defense's job to try and discredit them or their testimony. It was hard not to take it personally. The defense had used plenty of tricks to make McKinney squirm on the witness stand in the past, but he knew it was all part of the game. "Thanks," he said. "I don't consider you the enemy. I'll be here all day tomorrow if you want to stop by."

Nina Anderson chuckled. "It's your funeral. I'll see you tomorrow, around two."

"I'll be here." *Meeting with the enemy*, he thought. *Now I am in trouble*. As McKinney hung up the phone, a crumpled paper cup bounced off the back of his head and he turned to see his supervisor, Vivian Washington, a short, African-American woman with beaded hair extensions, holding a large evidence bag.

"I've got a present for you, McKinney."

"I'm suspicious of presents, Viv. My Aunt Claudia gave me a wool sweater for my tenth birthday, and I had to wear it every time she came to visit. It itched like hell."

Vivian rubbed her thumb and index finger together, representing the world's smallest violin. "Poor baby." She tossed him the evidence bag. "I've got a case for you. Another senior citizen was tortured and killed. This time an old lady, out in Bensenville."

"Killed how?"

"Shot. Back of the head."

"Was she tied to a chair?" McKinney asked.

"I don't know. Read the report. You can be our murdered seniors expert."

"Thanks, Viv."

He cleared off his desk, copied the case numbers from the bag to his notebook and opened the case file in the computer evidence-tracking system. Vivian had already entered the date and time that she had given McKinney the evidence bag, documenting the chain of custody. Without it the evidence was useless in court. Finally, he detached and read the police report that was stapled to the bag. The victim, Florence Burdett, was found on her kitchen floor, and like Arnold Drenon, she had ligature marks on her arms and chest but not on her back, an indication that she had been bound to a chair. The bag contained her clothing and a few pieces of broken glass, but what really got McKinney's attention was a notation that an impression of a shoeprint had been taken in the soft earth outside the woman's kitchen window. He looked at the evidence bag. It was marked one of two. The shoeprint cast was in the evidence vault.

McKinney sat back and looked at the wall over his computer monitor. There he had taped a poem by the Zen poet Issa to remind himself of the comic absurdity of trying to control human behavior with laws.

> *Simply trust*
> *Do not the petals flutter down?*
> *Just like that*

Why would anyone want to hurt a little old lady? He imagined her, perhaps someone's grandmother, tied to a chair and terrified. He had known only his paternal grandparents. When he was a child, his grandmother had baked pies in the kitchen of her small Chicago bungalow and he had been allowed to help. He loved to roll the dough out flat on the flour-dusted table. When his grandmother sifted the flour he would position himself so that the window was behind her. The falling cloud of flour would shimmer in the light. She had smelled like cinnamon and fried chicken and lavender. Now she lived in a gated community in Florida. He made a mental note to call her over the weekend.

He hoped this victim's family never found out that she'd been tortured. His job was to sort through the debris left by humans whose lives had been destroyed by violence. He tried to make himself immune to it, but he always felt sadness and indignation, as though the horrible thing had happened to someone he knew. He was acutely aware of that sadness now and distanced himself from it so it wouldn't influence his work. To be an effective scientist he had to be a dispassionate observer. This time, however, he was having a difficult time remaining detached. It wasn't so much the idea that someone would torture and kill an old lady—he had seen the results of cruelty let loose on women and children and babies. It had happened before and it would happen again, and there was nothing he could do to prevent it. What he could prevent was some poor schmo being railroaded by an ambitious attorney with no case. He could still see Phillips's cornered cat expression. If this murder was related to the other killing it would mean one of two things—either Phillips had a partner, or Phillips didn't do it.

He put on a disposable lab coat, hair cover, shoe covers, and latex gloves and took the evidence bag into one of the clean rooms—a large, well-lit room with nothing in it but a table and a roll of white butcher's paper. Contamination was his enemy, and he was careful to wipe down the table and the outside of the evidence bag with a 10 percent bleach solution. The room smelled like a swimming pool now.

He closed his eyes as an image came to him of Catherine, standing in waist-deep water, holding four-year-old Angelina while she kicked and paddled. Catherine had been determined Angelina would learn to swim. They took turns holding her, just at the water's surface, and walking her back and forth across the shallow end of the community pool. They did this every Saturday for six weeks. When McKinney thought Angelina had a grasp of the basics he let her go. She sank straight to the bottom of the pool. When they fished her out and she finished sputtering and coughing she looked at McKinney and said, "Don't get water in your nose, Dad. It hurts." The thought of it made him smile.

He tore off a sheet of paper and covered the table with it. Then he opened the bag and began the meticulous task of scraping down each article of clothing with a spatula. He hummed while he worked. People walking past the clean room were used to hearing "Catfish Blues" or "Hootchie Cootchie Man" being moaned off key.

Little bits of dirt, hair, and fibers slowly piled up on the paper. Some of the clothing was stained with blood or other body fluids and it all smelled of decay. The odor of chlorine mixed with rotting tissue was unpleasant, but McKinney was used to it. Finally, he poured the debris on the paper into an empty, plastic pillbox and laid out a new piece of paper. The victim's clothing had all been stuffed in the bag together, so there was a chance that some of the debris from her slacks had originally been on her blouse or vice versa. For that matter, it could have come from one of the police officers that found her or the M.E.'s assistant who had taken off her clothes and bagged them. McKinney hoped some of it was from the murderer.

It seemed obvious to McKinney that contact between two objects would likely cause a transfer of materials from one to the other, and he thought it strange that it hadn't been until the early twentieth century that Dr. Edmond Locard developed his famous Transfer Principle, the basis of McKinney's profession. Finally, he shook the empty bag over a clean sheet of paper. The resulting pile contained a number of small glass chips. He picked one up and inspected it. It wasn't window glass but he wasn't sure what it was. It looked like glass from a shattered tumbler, but there was no indication of a curve on any side. Had there been glass fragments collected from a suspect McKinney would have compared the striations and hackles along the edges, looking for a fracture match. There was a small brown smear on one chip. He separated that chip from the rest of the glass and sealed it in its own pillbox. He'd send it, along with any stained clothing, to the Biology Unit on the chance the smear was blood. He packed up everything else, made certain the bag was properly labeled, and locked it in his desk. His hands were damp and pruney from perspiration when he peeled off the latex gloves. He tossed the gloves in the trash, on top of the disposable protective wear, and went down the hall to the evidence vault to get the shoeprint cast.

An hour later he sat hunched over two photographs on his desk. They were digital images of the shoeprints from the Drenon killing and from the Burdett case that had just come in. He had flipped the image of the cast when he printed it out so that both prints were positives, facing the same direction. There were several points of comparison between them. They were both from a large-sized hiking boot, right foot, probably an eleven or twelve. The pattern of the lugs was the same and both prints showed wear on the instep, near the ball of the foot. The wearer probably put more weight on the inner sides of his feet when he walked, maybe due to a weak arch. Neither print showed the complete shoe pattern but the visible area in both showed a nice, unique characteristic, a damaged lug in the same position. There was a triangular slice missing from the top right corner of the lug, distinctive and unusual. McKinney was excited. *This shoe*, he thought, *was at both crime scenes*. Now all they had to do was find the shoe and its owner. The phone on McKinney's desk rang. He put down the two photographs and picked it up.

"McKinney here."

"Hi, Dad."

"Ciao, Bella...er, Angelina. What's up?"

"Oh, nothing. Just called to say hi. And, I'm making my famous pizza for dinner tonight."

"I love your pizza, but I have to work a little late tonight. You may have to eat without me."

Angelina was quiet for a moment. "But you have to come home," she said at last. "It's a special dinner."

"I'll be home as soon as I can, but I've got to get some of this done. What's so special about tonight?" There was another, longer, silence.

"I invited Mrs. Reyes to join us. She's bringing the dessert."

"Angelina, I've told you before, I'll start dating when I'm ready."

"It's not a date, Dad, it's just dinner. Besides, I saw you at the back window, watching her gardening. I know you think she's hot."

"That's not the point."

"Okay, we'll eat late. I'll call Mrs. Reyes and ask her to come around eight."

McKinney had tried not to think about romance since his wife's death. He changed the subject whenever the conversation turned toward dating and once snapped at a coworker who offered to introduce him to one of her friends. Dating would be accompanied by awkwardness and guilt. He wasn't ready for that.

"Listen..."

"She lost a husband too. I mean...anyway...she's lonely, and it'll just be a nice evening. Why don't you pick up a bottle of wine on your way home? A pinot noir would be nice."

"A pinot noir would be nice? You're sixteen. What do you know about pinot noir?"

"And try to get home in time to get cleaned up and change your shirt. I don't want you smelling like dead bodies at dinner."

"I never smell like dead bodies. Dead bodies go to the M.E.'s office, not the lab."

"You may not realize it, but sometimes you smell like dead bodies, and please don't talk about bugs tonight. I'm sure Mrs. Reyes doesn't want to learn about blowfly larva."

"You used to love talking about the bugs when you were little," he said. "Look, what if we don't get along? She's the building manager. She might cut off our hot water. I can't shower without hot water."

"You can shower at the gym. I've gotta go. I need to run to the store for sun-dried tomatoes. Don't forget the wine. Love ya."

"Me too."

"What's that, a guy thing? 'Me too'? You're embarrassed to tell your own daughter that you love her?"

McKinney held the phone at arms' length and shouted, "I love you, Angelina!" He brought the phone back to his ear.

"How was that?"

"You're the only one in the office, aren't you?"

"Well...yeah."

"Oh, Dad."

FIVE

Delroy's feet were tired from a morning of fruitless job hunting and hot from walking on the sun-baked pavement. The back of his shirt was sweaty and stuck to his skin. He didn't want to go back to the rooming house and face Lucille's disappointment when he told her he had once again failed to find work. He followed the route he had taken so many times before and slipped through a hole in the fence on the north end of the Century of Progress, near the 18th Street entrance.

The Fair had been open since May, and Delroy loved every bit of it, from Solomon's Temple to the Turtle Derby. It was a haven from the urban grit of Chicago. He could see the Sky-Ride from miles away. Its two towers rose six hundred and twenty-eight feet into the air. When lined up with the diner at 18th and Michigan they made a perfect beeline to the hole in the fence. Most days he would watch the lagoon divers or stare at the naked women on the murals in the Johns-Manville building. One in particular interested him. It was a beautiful woman with flowing red hair. She was being rescued from an ugly ogress by an angel. This was, somehow, supposed to represent a revolution in building materials for the modern home of 1933. Delroy saw it differently. To him it looked like Lucille, changing from the beautiful woman who stirred his loins and heart, into the nagging harpy who drove him from their bed every morning to trudge the city streets looking for work. He made a little money in June, helping to unload the trucks bringing merchandise and equipment to the Fair, but July had been lean. Their savings were almost gone. He had promised Lucille a better life than what they could plow from the Kentucky soil, and he had failed.

Delroy was filled with worry and wonderment and, consequently, he discovered a muse he didn't know he had—he started writing poetry. He wrote poems about Lucille's hair, Sally Rand the fan dancer, the beggars in front of Holy Name Cathedral, the cool wind blowing in off of Lake Michigan, and most of the attractions at the World's Fair. He even wrote one that was inspired by the Turtle Derby.

> *I watch the turtle races*
> *They're running mighty slow.*
> *Everyone is laughing*
> *But there's one thing you should know.*
> *It makes me sad to see them*
> *I think of Momma's turtle stew.*
> *It wasn't very tasty*
> *And it was kind of tough to chew.*
> *Sometimes she'd cook up squirrel*
> *Or possum in a pie,*
> *'Cause when you got three hungry kids*
> *There's nothing you won't try.*

Today he looked for a free indoor exhibit, out of the afternoon sun. He followed a group leaving the lagoon area into the Hall of Science and found himself in a large circular room with a high ceiling. It was cool and dimly lit and in the center stood the Transparent Man. Delroy hadn't seen this exhibit before, and he was amazed. The Transparent Man stood six feet tall and was made of clear plastic. You could see right through his skin to the bones and organs and blood vessels. He stood with his arms outstretched and his head raised, looking up, as if asking, "Why me, Lord?" The plaque in front of him said the Transparent Man had been made in Dresden, Germany at a cost of $10,000. It had taken German craftsmen eighteen months to make. That morning, Delroy had seen in the newspaper that the Nazis passed a law that anyone who was considered mentally or physically deficient could be sterilized by the government. He looked closely at the Transparent Man and noticed that he had all his parts. Delroy guessed that his sorrowful demeanor was due to being transparent and not because he was afraid of having his balls cut off. Even so, he felt a sense of kinship with him. He opened his arms and raised his face to the ceiling. When he lowered his head he was face to face with Freddie Barker.

Freddie and his family had moved into the rooming house the last week in June. They took the two front rooms on the second floor, across the hall from Delroy and Lucille. Freddie and his girlfriend, "Fat-Witted" Paula, had one room and his brother and mother shared the other. Sometimes a guy, whose name Delroy didn't know, spent the night. He once heard Freddie's brother call him "Creepy." This apparently upset the guy because he stormed out of the house and didn't come back for several days. Freddie seemed to like Delroy. Mrs. Finch, the landlady, had introduced them as good country folk, but there was something about Freddie that made Delroy nervous. Whenever Freddie talked his voice would get loud and his eyes would get big. Most of the time you could see the whites of his eyes all the way around the colored part. This was particularly evident when his brother was around. Freddie's brother never raised his voice and his eyes seemed to be in a perpetual squint. Unlike Freddie, who laughed a lot, his brother never even smiled. Lucille and Mrs. Finch seemed to like Freddie because he laughed so easily and was good to his mother, but Delroy rarely understood what Freddie was laughing at. He just thought the whole family was odd.

"Hey, Dell." Freddie nodded his head toward the Transparent Man. "You talkin' to this guy? 'Cause if you is I'll be glad to call the little men in the white coats."

"Oh, hey, Freddie. Naw. Just takin' in the sights before I go home."

"Home. You mean Finch's flytrap. My mattress is as lumpy as her pancakes."

"Yeah. Ours is, too. Her cooking ain't that bad though."

"Ma's is better. Hey, how's that little redheaded chickie of yours. Can she cook?"

"Lucille? She tries. We've got that kitchenette in our room. Just between you and me though, don't ever drink her coffee. You'll be blind for three days."

As they talked, Freddie took Delroy by the elbow and walked him out of the Hall of Science and back onto the midway. He did this so smoothly that Delroy didn't notice until they were weaving through the perspiring crowd. They stopped in front of the Schlitz Garden restaurant. A cool breeze drifted in from the lake as Freddie put his arm around Delroy's shoulder. The breeze carried the smell of the dead alewives that had washed up on the lakeshore.

"C'mon. All this yak is makin' me thirsty. I'll buy you a beer. A real beer, no more of that watered-down crap. Happy days are here again, eh?"

Four beers and a dozen oysters later Delroy wasn't feeling much better about his financial situation, but his reservations about Freddie had dissolved in a haze of malt and foam.

"Times are tough, eh, Dell?"

"I haven't had any work in three weeks." He wiped his nose on his sleeve. "Some husband I turned out to be. I promised Lucille I'd take care of her but if I don't find something soon I'll have to send her back to her people in Kentucky. I don't know if I could stand that."

"That'd be a goddam shame. Tell me somethin', Dell, you ever hear of this fella, Dillinger?"

"The bank robber? Sure, I've heard of him. Why?"

"What do you think of his business?"

"You mean robbing banks?"

"Yeah, robbing banks. What do you think?"

"I dunno. Times are tough. I guess some folks'll do about anything to keep from starving."

Freddie smiled. "You don't think it's wrong?"

"Sure it's wrong, but it's wrong that decent folks can't feed their kids while the men what run these big companies are getting rich. Times are tough, that's all."

"Would you do it?"

"Shoot. I'm no robber. I wouldn't know how, even if I wanted to."

Freddie leaned closer to Delroy. "I'm going to tell you something, Dell, but you have to swear you won't tell nobody else."

"I swear."

"Me and some other fellas have been robbing banks for a while now and whoever said crime don't pay was a chump."

Delroy was suddenly as sober as if he'd been hit in the face with a bucket of ice water. He knew that what Freddie was telling him was important. Looking at his crazy eyes, he had no doubt that it was true. His palms began to sweat.

"You ever kill anyone?"

"Only bulls, Dell, and the ones I shot would've killed me if they'd had the chance. It was unavoidable."

"Oh."

"How'd you like to make yourself an easy couple of hundred bucks so's you don't have to ship your chickie back to Kentucky?"

"I can't rob a bank, Freddie. I'm just a farmer. I wouldn't be any good at it."

"I don't mean that you'd do any of the rough stuff. We just need a lookout man is all. One of our boys got clipped on the last job, and he's laid up for a while. We're going out to Vandalia in a couple of days, and we just need you to keep an eye out for the bulls while we're inside. If you see anything, you signal me and then walk away."

"I don't know..."

"No one will connect you with the job, and you get a couple of C-notes for about fifteen minutes work. It's a sweet deal."

"A couple of C-notes, huh? That's—"

"Tell you what, Dell. We'll make it three hundred."

Delroy had been fiddling with his empty glass, but now he stopped and stared at Freddie Barker. Three hundred dollars was a whole helluva lot of money. Mrs. Finch had been good about the rent, but they owed her for the last two months. Delroy had taken to listening at the door to make certain she wasn't in the hall before leaving the apartment. Here was his chance to be the husband Lucille deserved. If there was any cash left over maybe he would bring her to the fair. He'd snuck her in through the hole in the fence a few times, but all they could afford to do was wander around and look at the free exhibits.

"How long would we be gone?"

"Just a couple of days. How about it?"

"I'll have to come up with a good story for Lucille."

"Tell her you're sick of that dog drool she calls coffee. Tell her you're going out for a cup and you'll be back in three days."

SIX

The cut was several days old, but the memory was fresh in Gilbert's mind and it worried him. The Bensenville job had started smoothly. He made certain the old lady was alone by peering through her kitchen window. He talked her door open with a story about finding his daughter's house and wouldn't she take a look at the address on this envelope that he couldn't quite make out. He slugged her as soon as she opened the door, and by the time she came around he had her tied to a chair in the flower-filled kitchen. The whole house, he noticed, was filled with fresh-cut flowers. He found the sickly-sweet smell almost overpowering.

He sat across from her, dangling the little gun in her face. She answered his questions readily and winced whenever he moved. He enjoyed this and began to supplement his interrogation with sudden movements, just to see her jump.

Florence Burdett was kind of proud of her big sister's association with the famous Barker/Karpis gang, and she told Gilbert everything she could remember. Wynona had told her all the stories of how she and Harry Campbell had been on the run from the feds and how they had shot their way out of a trap. Ma and Freddie Barker were killed by the FBI in Florida and Wynona and Harry ran with Alvin Karpis and his girlfriend to Atlantic City. They holed up in the Danmore Hotel there, but the manager ratted them out to the G-men. There was a knock early in the morning and, when Karpis opened the door, he found himself surrounded by cops. He talked loud enough to tip Harry, who was listening at the door in the next room.

Harry flung open the door and waded into them, screaming at the top of his lungs, his machine gun chattering. One of the cops was wounded and the others retreated down the stairs, giving the foursome enough time to slip out the back way. In the excitement Karpis's girlfriend was hit in the leg. She was pregnant and couldn't run, so Harry and Karpis went to get the car while Wynona stayed with her. The feds nabbed them before the boys got back with the car. The girls each got seven years.

Wynona spent the rest of her life telling that story to anyone who'd listen, but if she knew anything about the gold she hadn't told her sister. Florence knew nothing about it, but she did know the whereabouts of another of the gang's gun molls, Gertrude Billiter. Gertrude was the young girl Harry Campbell married after abandoning Wynona in Atlantic City. Harry met her when he and Karpis were hiding out in Toledo, Ohio. Wynona was furious when she found out and, after she was released from prison, tracked Gertrude down to have it out, but with Harry doing life in Alcatraz there wasn't really much for them to fight about. They became friends. Florence didn't much care for her older sister's friends. They all seemed set in their ways, and Gertrude was no exception. Despite her gangster past, Florence found Gertrude to be rather dull.

Gertrude lived out in Aurora, and Florence gladly gave Gilbert the address. Then the phone rang. Gilbert was standing with his back to the phone and, startled, he spun around, smashing a rectangular glass vase with the gun in his hand. This upset him so much he picked up his bag, put his gun to Florence's head, fired twice, and walked out of the house without saying another word. She had told him all she knew.

It wasn't until he got home that he realized he'd cut his finger. It was a small cut. He checked the latex glove he'd worn; there was no blood on the outside. Was there any blood, he worried, in the old lady's house?

"Fuck!" he shouted.

He walked over to the apartment's little kitchenette and took a beer from the refrigerator. The cold beer felt good on his hot throat. He decided to make dinner. He opened one end of a can of beef stew with a can opener, flipped the can over, and drove a paring knife into the other end. The hole released the pressure on the inside of the can, and its goopy contents slid out into the pot on the stove.

"All right. Okay. There's no reason to panic." He threw the knife across the room and smiled when it stuck in the wall above the television.

"Let's just stick to the fucking plan and find the fucking gold." He lit the burner under the pot of stew and walked back to the desk to study his map. "Now where the hell is Aurora?"

SEVEN

Instead of hitting the snooze button McKinney had accidentally turned off his alarm clock. He liked to start each day with a leisurely breakfast and some tai chi practice, but oversleeping this morning caused him to miss both. He just had time to shower and dress before leaving for work. He raced past Angelina, who was finishing the last of her yogurt and cereal at the kitchen table.

"You know," she said, "breakfast is the most important meal of the day."

He grabbed a banana on his way out the back door.

He was going through the trace evidence he'd collected from Florence Burdett's clothing when Nina Anderson arrived at the lab. The receptionist phoned shortly after lunch to let him know she was downstairs in the lobby. He locked the evidence in a drawer, hung up his lab coat and went down to meet her. He signed her in, gave her a visitor's badge and led her to the small conference room he called the "fish bowl" because one of its walls was made of glass. This was where he usually met with prosecutors or detectives who wanted to discuss the physical evidence in a case. On rare occasions he met there with defense attorneys.

He bought them both coffee from a vending machine, then sat across the walnut veneer table and watched her arrange the copies of his notes on the table between them. Instead of the suit he'd seen in court she wore a silky, green blouse that matched her eyes and a skirt that revealed nicely rounded calves. She appeared nervous. She picked up the papers, tapped the stack on the table to square them up and laid them back down, checking to make sure the bottom of the stack was parallel to the edge of the table.

"First of all, thank you for giving me your notes," she said. "Because of you I was able to get a continuance. I've got a few more weeks to try and come up with a defense for this young man."

No wonder Jameson was so mad. "Don't mention it." Now *he* was getting nervous. He caught himself tapping his foot.

"The only other report I got was from the medical examiner," she continued. "The cause and approximate time of death. There was nothing in your report about blood or semen or any kind of DNA evidence."

"No, I only do trace evidence."

"So you don't deal with blood or fingerprints? That's done in a different unit?"

"Right. I examine evidence like paint, hair, fibers, glass, gunshot residue, soil. All types of microscopic evidence."

"So you're a micro—, a microscopic analyst?"

McKinney chuckled. "Microscopical, I guess, with the A L. If I was microscopic I'd be really small." He held up his hand, thumb and forefinger close together. Realizing the implication, he blushed.

Nina Anderson smiled and looked down at her hands, folded on her lap. McKinney remembered that he had wanted to see her smile the day he handed her his case notes. The smile was warm and almost bashful and made her face glow. He was not disappointed. "Um…I also do physical comparisons and some forensic entomology, though there's not much call for that."

"Entomology?" she asked. "Insect stuff?"

"Yeah. My undergrad was in zoology, and I studied bugs with Peter Williamson, the best forensic entomologist around.

They help me determine things like time of death or location, if a body's been moved. I don't get to use it very often, though."

"You gave me your notes about the dog hairs, footprints, and gunshot residue. Why didn't I get reports from other analysts, the people who did the blood or the fingerprints?"

"Because," McKinney said, "they couldn't get a match from your client. I checked the other case files in the computer. All the blood collected was from the victim. The Fingerprint Unit ran a couple of prints through the AFIS database, but didn't get any hits. All they could do was rule a few people out—the crime scene techs, Mr. Drenon, your client. The prints could belong to Drenon's friends or relatives or a cleaning lady. That's why I thought it was important for you to have my notes. There isn't any physical evidence linking your client to the murder."

"Is that normal procedure—to check the findings of other units in the lab?"

"No, I guess I was curious. I wanted to know what kind of person would torture and kill a little old man, so I checked to see if anyone else was able to find anything. Did anybody see Phillips going in or out of the victim's house?"

"No."

"Then why did he confess? I got the impression from the state's attorney that he might be mentally handicapped in some way."

"Phillips is autistic. He spent most of his youth in a mental health facility. On one of his visits home, when he was about twelve years old, he wandered into Mr. Drenon's yard. Drenon chased him out, Phillips threw a rock and hit Drenon in the arm, so Phillips's parents decided he was dangerous and promptly sent him back to the facility. That's what he thought he was confessing to. Something he did over a decade ago."

McKinney watched her start to fidget again. She repeated

the same paper-straightening ritual. When she finished he casually picked up the top sheet of his report, looked at it, and set it down again, slightly askew. He sensed her hesitation but, finally, she reached out and lined the page up with the others, running her finger along the edge of the stack to even it out.

"I have some obsessive-compulsive behavior traits," she said. "It's not full-blown OCD, though. I don't need medication, but I see a therapist. I guess I can relate to Phillips a little. Maybe feel some empathy for him."

"Empathy is fine, but do you believe he's innocent?"

"Just like in your job, Mr. McKinney, that's not supposed to matter. Every defendant is guaranteed the right to counsel under the Constitution." She pulled her hands back from the sheaf of papers and folded them in her lap. She looked down at a ragged thumbnail. "I pretty much have to believe in my clients' innocence these days. It's no secret that one of them killed a little girl after I got him released. I couldn't take another case like that. I still have trouble sleeping. Yes, I think Phillips is innocent."

"Have you talked to the investigator?"

She laughed. "Detective Barger. He told me the officers picked Phillips up in the alley behind the victim's house. They were responding to a call from a neighbor who saw someone suspicious come out of Mr. Drenon's back door. Phillips confessed to the murder that night, and Barger closed the file. I've called him so often he's sick of me. He figures he got the right guy and now he won't return my calls. You're the only one, besides me, who thinks Phillips is innocent."

McKinney shook his head. "Whoa, hold on. I didn't say I thought he was innocent. I can't even say that he wasn't at the crime scene, only that there's no evidence to put him there."

"But you're willing to help me, aren't you?"

"At this point, the only way to show a jury he wasn't there is with an alibi. What about his parents?"

"They aren't exactly on his side. I don't think they ever got used to having a child who's 'different.' Remember, they're the ones who sent him away in the first place. Until a year ago he was living in a halfway house. I got the impression that bringing him home had mostly been a financial decision. Anyway, they were out of town that night. Las Vegas. They'd left him alone for the weekend with a cupboard full of microwave soups."

"Well, I don't think there's much I can do," McKinney said. "But yesterday I received the evidence from the murder case of an elderly woman and it has some similar features to Mr. Drenon's murder. I'll contact the investigators on both cases and see if I can get them interested in looking at yours a little closer."

A movement out of the corner of his eye caught his attention and he turned to see Director Roberts, standing at the conference room window, staring in at him. *Oh, here we go*, he thought. McKinney stood and extended his hand to the attorney, indicating the end of the interview. She stood up and shook his hand, holding on just a bit longer than necessary, McKinney thought.

"Will you keep me informed about the other case?" she asked. "At least let me know if the detectives think there's a connection."

"I will," he promised.

When he opened the door to the hallway Roberts was gone. McKinney escorted the lawyer out as quickly as he could.

EIGHT

Delroy stood inside the Citizens Bank of Vandalia, Illinois, at the bank's front window, and wished he were anywhere else. It was the middle of the afternoon, well past the lunch hour, and through the brass bars on the window he could see that the street was empty, except for a few small children chasing a ball. The afternoon sun passing through the bars striped the oiled wood floor behind him, but Delroy didn't notice. His partners were in the back, robbing the bank, but that wasn't his concern. His job was to pay attention to the street. There was a lump in his throat, a knot in his stomach, and his palms were sweaty.

He wore an old double-breasted suit he'd inherited from his father and a felt fedora, pulled low over his eyes. He held a large red apple up near his mouth in an unnatural pose. Whenever he turned his head to survey the street his hand would move with it, forward and back, forward and back. He looked like a nervous dignitary in a parade, waving at the crowd. His instructions were simple. If he saw a cop he was to drop the apple. Freddie would be keeping an eye on him from the back and if he saw the apple drop they would abort the job and walk to the car, calmly and quietly. They weren't taking any chances. Of course, if the cops were heading toward the bank he was to shout so they could all hear. In that case they'd make a run for it.

The day before they'd all piled into the big, twelve-cylinder Auburn sedan and driven the escape route, east across the Kaskaskia River, switched cars at Brownstown, then north toward Chicago. The mood was less than jovial. Delroy sat in the back, sandwiched between Monty Bolton and "Shotgun" George Zeigler, two hoods who'd been with the Barker/Karpis gang a month ago when they kidnapped William Hamm, Jr., the beer magnate. Bolton still wasn't satisfied with his cut of the ransom money and, every time he mentioned it, Zeigler would pat the ominous bulge under his coat and lean across Delroy's lap to comment, "You think I got too much, Bolton? Why don't you try and take some back?" This would start Freddie Barker and Alvin Karpis shouting at them from the front seat until Zeigler and Bolton shut up. They'd ride along in strained silence for another thirty miles or so, and then Bolton would start again. *How the hell*, thought Delroy, *are these guys ever going to work together to rob a bank?* But that morning there was no arguing. Zeigler and Bolton were all business as they reviewed the rough drawing of the bank Karpis had supplied and checked their guns.

Delroy entered the bank at exactly three o'clock and took up his position at a desk in front of the window. He pretended to fill out a deposit slip while he looked around for cops, then he held up his apple. The four stickup men entered as a unit, drew their guns, and went to work. Karpis went over the counter first. He positioned himself by the back door to keep anyone from leaving that way. This also gave him a clean view of the two clerks that Bolton had put on the floor. Zeigler grabbed the manager and walked him over to a locked cage filled with mailbags. Freddie stayed close to the counter where he could keep an eye on both the front and back, and still see Delroy at the window.

Delroy continued to look up and down the street but his mind wasn't on his work. He was busy worrying. First he worried about Lucille. What would she say if she knew what he was doing? What would happen to her if he was caught or killed? Then he worried about the children playing in the street. Were they in danger? What if somebody started shooting? He tried to will them away from the bank. *Get out of here*, he thought. *Go play somewhere else.* A noise from the back caught his attention, and he inched back from the window so he could see what was happening behind him. Freddie was looking at the locked cage and grinning. Delroy followed his gaze to where George Zeigler stood, talking to the manager.

The manager was a plump little man who wore an Elks' tooth on his vest and sleeve garters on his arms. The garters were tight and his fingers looked like pink sausages. There was a name tag pinned to his vest that identified him as Oswald Green. He tried to stall Zeigler with a story about not knowing where the key to the walk-in cage was kept. Zeigler hit him in the mouth with his gun. Oswald swore through the ruins of his teeth.

"Damn it! You didn't need to do that."

Zeigler grinned and raised his gun again. "Are you gonna open this cage or not?"

Oswald tried to fish a key out of his vest pocket, but fear and anger made his chubby fingers clumsy. Finally, Zeigler slapped his hand away, got the key, and opened the cage himself. He and Bolton knew exactly which bags to take. Karpis left his post and herded the two frightened clerks into the cage with Oswald. Zeigler locked the door and tossed the key across the room. He grinned at the little manager.

"So long, Oswald. Thanks for all the money."

Oswald yanked open the top drawer of a file cabinet and pulled out an old German revolver.

Blood sprayed from his swollen lips as he screamed at Zeigler, "I'll show you, tough guy. You don't hit me like that."

He got off one shot, nicking Zeigler in the calf. Zeigler swore, turned on his heel and shot Oswald in the chest. Oswald looked surprised for a moment, then collapsed. One of the clerks screamed, and the three stickup men grabbed the bags and ran. Delroy quickly turned back to the window. The street was still empty. Freddie Barker shouted as he scrambled across the counter. "Let's go! Move it, Dell!"

Out in the street they piled into the Auburn. Bolton pushed Delroy into the car and slid in behind him as it lurched away from the curb. Delroy was still holding his apple.

Zeigler was gripping his calf, trying to stop the blood that dribbled between his fingers.

"I should've shot that fucking Kraut as soon as I got the key. This is what I get for being a nice guy."

Bolton laughed. "Did you see the look on that guy's face when you shot him? That was beautiful."

Delroy was looking out the window as they sped past the other cars on the road. *Karpis is driving too fast*, he thought. *They're going to attract the cops. Why are they laughing? They shot someone, maybe killed him. Why don't they shut up?* He couldn't tell Lucille. She'd be as ashamed of him as he was of himself.

"Aren't we going too fast?" he asked.

Bolton turned and looked at Delroy as if he was seeing him for the first time. "What's the matter, Petunia? Afraid the coppers are going to get you?"

Freddie looked back over the seat at them. "Leave him alone. He did okay. Three hundred bucks for a lookout is cheap. Dell, either eat that apple or throw it out the window. You look stupid holding it up like that."

Delroy took a bite. It tasted mealy, but he forced himself to eat it. It was evidence and had to be destroyed. The taste stayed in his mouth all the way to Chicago. The inside of the car smelled like gunpowder and sweat. He had to concentrate to keep from retching. The next day he wrote a poem about his adventure.

> *An apple a day keeps the doctor away,*
> *That's what they tell you in school.*
> *But if you go on a job,*
> *where your pals kill and rob,*
> *You're just a no-account fool.*

NINE

Gilbert referred to the restaurant as the International House of Rug Rats because it was usually packed with mothers and their screaming infants. He ate there anyway because it was walking distance from his apartment, habitually sitting in the same maroon vinyl booth under the Greek islands travel poster. The waitresses all knew him and today it was Doris— little tits, big ass, thumb in his hash browns. He liked her, though. She laughed at his jokes and always called him "Hon" or "Dear."

It was an obituary notice that caused Gilbert to postpone his trip to Aurora. As a child, he had watched his father pore over the obituaries every morning at breakfast, looking for leads to old gangsters. Now he did the same, scouring the paper in between bites of egg and toast.

Over the years he'd developed a system. He would tear the death notices out of all the papers and scan them for last name and date of birth, circling anyone who might be old enough to remember Karpis or the Barkers. His best bet would have been Karpis's women, Dorothy Slayman or Dolores Delaney, but they were long gone. Freddie Barker's girlfriend, Paula "Fat-Witted" Harmon died in an asylum but he'd traced her younger brother to a small bungalow on Chicago's northwest side. The brother, Arnold Drenon, endured several hours of torture that had turned up no pertinent information. Gilbert had even shot his dogs. But the old man either didn't know anything or wouldn't tell, so, finally, Gilbert killed him. That he had enjoyed killing him came as a surprise. He noted these new feelings but didn't spend much time analyzing them. He preferred to think of himself as a businessman. Today, the very first obituary notice he circled caught his eye.

> *Irene Gwinn, formerly Goetz née Kelly, preceded in death by her loving husband Sidney; loving mother to Roger (Margaret), fond grandmother to Patrick. Mrs. Gwinn was a member of St. Bernardine Parish, Forest Park. She was a graduate of the University of Illinois. She worked for the USO during World War II. Visitation Thursday, from 3 to 9 p.m. at Pulaski Brothers Funeral Home in Oak Park. In lieu of flowers, memorials may be made to the Chicago Public Library Foundation.*

Gilbert almost dropped his coffee—*formerly Goetz.* "Shotgun" George Ziegler's real name had been Fred Goetz, and he was married to a woman named Irene. Ziegler/Goetz had not only been a member of the Barker/Karpis gang, he had also been one of the triggermen at the St. Valentine's Day massacre. It didn't make sense, she'd be ancient by now, but it was too big a coincidence to ignore. He read the notice again—*loving mother to Roger.* Tomorrow was the visitation, and Roger would probably be there. He would have a little chat with Roger.

He tore the notice out and, smiling, slipped it into his shirt pocket. He felt four million dollars richer. Those gold coins were going to mean a lot of things for him. No more walk-up studio apartments overlooking noisy bus stops. No more poking around in other people's houses looking for jewelry and coin collections. Mostly it meant no more feeling like a failure. He was going to travel. He closed his eyes and imagined himself sitting in a beach chair, looking out at the deep, blue

Mediterranean and sipping martinis. In the chair next to him was a blonde woman in one of those one-piece swimsuits, the kind with some of the material cut out on the sides. And her fingernails would be cut short, manicured, but with clear nail polish. Classy. *It doesn't really matter where I go*, he thought, *as long as I'm gone*. He would finally get away from the stink of the low-class life he had grown up in. He would get away from motels with hourly rates and bus stations in the middle of the night and canned meals. He would get away from everything that reminded him of his father.

The waitress stopped at his table to refill his coffee. "How're the eggs, hon?"

"Doris," he said, "these are the best eggs I've ever tasted."

There was a crowd at the Pulaski Brothers Funeral Home in Oak Park. Irene Gwinn, formerly Goetz, had been well liked. Gilbert decided this would work in his favor. It might make it harder to get Roger alone but at least he wouldn't stand out. He could blend. He wore a dark gray suit and a maroon tie. He could easily pass for a mourner or one of the funeral home staff. The only concession to the task at hand was his crepe-soled shoes. They weren't quite dressy enough, but if he needed to run he didn't want to risk slipping on the terrazzo-tiled floor. He entered the viewing room just as a priest began leading the seated mourners in prayer. Gilbert pretended to sign the guest book, then took a seat in the last row. He bowed his head but kept his eyes open, surveying the room and calculating his odds. The room was an assemblage of pastel colors and rococo furnishings, with plaster scrolls and ribbons on the walls near the ceiling. The collection of old women who had come to pay their respects would feel right at home but it gave Gilbert the creeps. It was like being laid out in some weird museum.

There were ten rows of folding chairs set up, the first eight rows filled with mourners. In addition to himself there was only one other person in the last row, a man with a carnation in his lapel, probably the funeral director. Beyond the seated mourners was the priest, standing at a small podium, and beyond him was the casket, surrounded by flowers. Most of the mourners were old ladies, and the room smelled heavily of cologne and talcum powder. In the first row sat a middle-aged couple, the man sniffling into a handkerchief. He was chubby and balding, and what hair he had left was gray at the temples. He wore the ugliest suit Gilbert had ever seen. It was light blue and made of some synthetic material that reflected the yellow fluorescent lighting in the room. This, he supposed, was Roger, the dead woman's son. When the priest ended the prayer he gestured to the man, who stepped up to the podium and addressed the mourners. Gilbert didn't listen to all of the speech. He was still studying the layout of the room and had decided that the door to the left of the casket offered some possibilities. The end of the speech, though, drew his attention and confirmed the man's identity.

"My mother," Roger said, "was the best mother a son could have, and I know she would have liked nothing better than to be with her savior. She's there now. She's living in a city made of crystal and emerald and jasper. She's living with Jesus in his city on the mountain."

There was a dramatic pause before the last sentence and a short, dry sob at the end. Gilbert almost laughed. *Just the way I would have delivered it,* he thought, *if I was trying to convince people I was grief-stricken. He's probably been anticipating his inheritance for years.* Gilbert recognized the description of the crystal city from the Book of Revelation.

His one, brief stint in prison had been spent with nothing to read but a handful of magazines and a Bible. "A foolish son is a grief to his father," he recalled, "and bitterness to her that bare him." Gilbert stepped outside as the priest was returning to the podium. He drove his old, maroon Taurus around to the alley and parked it near the door he had noticed in the back of the viewing room. He released the trunk latch, then went back inside and sat down to wait. He put his hand in his pocket and, while he sat, stroked the little Beretta. Its cold presence gave him confidence.

When the service was over, and most of the mourners had paid their respects and left, Gilbert approached the casket and stood, staring down at the shrunken body in the lavender dress and trying to look sad. Roger came over and stood next to him. Gilbert looked up and extended his hand. "She was a fine woman. You're Roger, aren't you? Your mother spoke of you often."

The man took Gilbert's hand. He was so wrapped up in his role as the grieving son that he didn't think to ask Gilbert who he was or how he knew his mother.

"She was the best mother a son could have," he repeated.

Gilbert placed his other hand on Roger's shoulder and turned him toward the back door. "You need to come with me. I have something to tell you about your mother, and I'd like to do it in private."

They had covered half the distance to the door before Roger realized something was wrong. He looked at Gilbert for the first time. Gilbert gripped his hand harder, pulling the man close and draping his arm across his shoulders. "You can tell me here, mister," Roger said. "No one can hear us."

Gilbert smiled at him and patted his shoulder in a reassuring way. "That's right. No one can hear us. I need you to step outside with me for a minute. I just want to talk but I'm warning you, I have a gun in my pocket. Keep quiet and cooperate, or I'll kill you and your wife." They had continued to walk and were almost at the door. Gilbert released his hand. "Open the door," he said. As they stepped into the alley he spun Roger to face him and punched him, hard, in the solar plexus. Roger gasped and bent forward at the waist. Gilbert bent low enough to get his shoulder under Roger's chest and his hand behind his knee. He straightened quickly and tipped him into the open trunk. He looked down at the mixture of pain and bewilderment on Roger's face. "Watch your fingers," he said, and slammed the lid closed.

TEN

McKinney nervously fingered the little figurine on Detective Moses Boadu's desk. It was Curly, from The Three Stooges, dressed in golfing attire. Detective Boadu also had a golf ball tape dispenser, a Tiger Woods calendar, and a coffee mug proclaiming his membership in the Frustrated Golfers Club. McKinney looked at the figurine in his hand. "Nyuk, nyuk," he muttered. He looked around the office. It held several other desks and, on the far wall, there was a window that looked out on an alley. The walls were painted an institutional green that had been darkened by years of cigarette smoke. These days, government employees, including Bensenville police officers, were supposed to go outside to smoke, but the butt-filled ashtray on the detective's desk indicated the rule wasn't strictly adhered to.

McKinney replaced the figurine just as Detective Boadu came back from the file room. He tossed a manila folder on the desk in front of McKinney and wedged himself into his chair. The detective had the blackest skin McKinney had ever seen, and he packed well over two hundred pounds onto his five-foot, five-inch frame. He wore a short-sleeved shirt and a bright blue striped tie. Typical well-dressed detective, McKinney thought. "You like golf, I take it," he said.

"Love it. I'd play every day if I could."

"I used to play, but I was so bad I felt like I should wipe my fingerprints off the clubs."

Boadu chuckled politely and opened the folder on the desk. "Here's the file on Miss Burdett. Your report's in there, too.

Case is still open but I haven't got squat to go on. No one was seen going in or out of her house, and none of her friends can think of anyone who hated her. The place was pretty torn up but we can't tell if anything was stolen. Didn't find any valuables, so I assume she was robbed—but the torture? Unless she had a hidey-hole full of cash or jewelry, why torture a little old lady? That was some cold shit."

"I don't know," McKinney said. He flipped through the thin file. "But that's what I want to find out. I told you about the Drenon killing over the phone. They're just too similar to be a coincidence. And then there are the shoeprints."

"Yeah," the detective said, "the shoeprints." He chuckled. "Our man's pretty slick, gets in and out easy enough, picks up his shell casings and doesn't leave any fingerprints lyin' around, but he wears the same shoes. I'd be willing to bet he still has 'em, too."

"Why do you say 'our man'? A strong woman could've easily overpowered both of the victims."

"What size shoe made those prints?" Boadu asked.

McKinney checked the file for his notes. "Eleven or twelve."

"A man. So, what do you want me to do? I got no suspects, no leads. There haven't been any home invasions in that neighborhood. No unsolved burglaries, other than a few garage break-ins, so we can't fit it into any kind of pattern. Just looks like some kinda random thing."

"I'd like you to talk to Detective Barger, the investigator on the Drenon case. Maybe if the two of you compare notes, you'll come up with something. At least you can get him to take another look."

"Sure, I know Dave Barger. I used to be a Chicago cop before I moved out to Bensenville. I'll call him."

McKinney relaxed a little. He had done what he could for Phillips. Whatever obligation he had to see justice done had been passed on to Moses Boadu. It was out of his hands now. He could feel his shoulders relax. He was happy as he drove home to get ready for his date.

The mirror was steamy from his shower and McKinney wiped it with the heel of his hand. He turned his face to look at one side and then the other. He wasn't crazy about what he saw. "You're getting a little wrinkly there, McKinney." He sang a few bars of "How Many More Years," but he couldn't imitate Howlin' Wolf's gravelly voice. It just made his throat hurt.

Angelina's pizza dinner with Carla Reyes had turned out to be a lot of fun. McKinney was surprised to discover that, in addition to being their building manager, she was an artist. After a few awkward moments, the three of them had started trading silly jokes, and soon they were giggling at anything. Carla wasn't a dainty laugher. She had the kind of laugh that got her whole body involved, and McKinney found himself trying hard to make her laugh. The look on his face when she asked him out on a date had produced the biggest guffaw of the evening. She and Angelina laughed so hard they ended up crying. McKinney had no choice but to say yes.

He picked up a hand mirror and held it over the back of his head to get a look at his thinning hair. "Aw, crap." He should never have agreed to go on this date. He was worrying about his appearance, something he hadn't done in years. He didn't need this. He had more important things to think about. He was glad to be finished with the Phillips case, though. He had already gone far beyond his job description. He was just supposed to analyze the evidence. It was up to the detectives and the state's attorney to make use of his analysis. Despite that, he couldn't get Phillips out of his head, and he didn't know why. Something about him... He put the mirror down when he heard the phone ring, and a moment later there was a knock at the bathroom door.

"Dad. Phone. It's Great-grandma Lucy."

He pulled on his pants, shuffled out to the kitchen, and took the phone from Angelina's outstretched hand.

"Grandma, how are you? How are things in sunny Florida?"

"Too sunny, darlin'. If I go outside I'll turn into a cancer. When are you and that pretty little girl of yours coming to see me?"

"You know I was just thinking about you the other day." He decided not to tell her it was because women her age were being murdered in their homes. "We should come down. I've got some vacation time left. Maybe in the fall, when the asphalt in your driveway is a little less molten."

"Oh, I wish you could come sooner. When does Angelina go back to school?"

"Oh, yeah, I don't know. Let me look into that and I'll let you know. So, what have you been doing?"

"Well, I still have my ladies' club. We go out to lunch every Sunday after church."

"That sounds like fun."

"Well, you know how some of these old ladies are. They can suffer in silence louder than anyone."

Suddenly Angelina was standing in front of him holding up a piece of notebook paper on which she had written BIRTHDAY 95!!

"Say," McKinney said. "Don't you have a birthday coming up? Your ninety-fifth, if I recall correctly."

"Yes, darlin', at the end of this month."

"Well, that changes everything. Of course, we'll come down to celebrate."

"That's wonderful, dear. Tell Angelina I said, 'Thank you.' Us girls have got to stick together, you know."

"Uh, huh. Here, you tell her. Bye. Love you." He handed the phone to his smirking daughter and went to finish dressing.

He put on a black silk t-shirt and khaki chinos. Carla had agreed to go to his favorite club, the Cermak Lounge. It was a small, squat, concrete blockhouse on the South Side, just over the line, in Berwyn. The interior wasn't much more than a bar and a stage, with a few posters of aging bluesmen sharing the walls with neon beer signs. The regulars were a mixed lot—blues aficionados, drunks, and walk-ins from the White Castle next door—none of the tourists or college kids who frequented the downtown clubs. It offered sticky floors, cheap booze, and some of the best musicians in Chicago. He knew it wasn't really the place to take a woman on a first date but, if she couldn't tolerate a real blues club, there wouldn't be any point in a second date. Still, he wanted to look nice. It was too hot out to wear a sport coat, but he decided to bring one along. They were going to eat first and, if it was cool in the restaurant, he could wear it during dinner.

Our mating rituals aren't much different from those of insects, he thought. The nursery web spider takes his date to dinner, too, though that's mostly so she won't eat him while he's mounting her. As an afterthought he took off his old, beat-up gym shoes and slipped into loafers.

He wondered if his daughter's efforts to get him to start dating might be as much for her own sake as for his. McKinney worried that he was robbing her of some important part of her adolescence. Sixteen was a difficult age for any girl. She shouldn't have to take care of her father, too. When he heard the knocking on the front door he almost ran to answer it but caught himself and slowed down in the living room. *I guess I am a little nervous*, he thought.

Carla leaned up, gave him a peck on the cheek and twirled as she entered so McKinney could admire her outfit. She wore a colorful print skirt that flowed with her body when she moved and a billowy white cotton blouse. She wore sandals but, even in heels, she would have been inches shorter than he was. When she stopped twirling she pushed a lock of black hair out of her face. The big poodle got up from the floor, where he'd been napping, and pushed the top of his head into her hand.

"Hendrix, settle down," McKinney said.

Carla scratched the dog behind an ear, and when he flopped over onto his back, she bent to rub his stomach.

"You look lovely, Carla."

"Why, thank you, Sean," she chuckled. "So do you."

McKinney was surprised. At work he was just "McKinney." No one had called him by his first name in a long time. After Catherine died he had closed himself off from family and friends. The nonstop stream of sympathy and advice had the opposite of its intended effect. It made him realize how alone he felt without her. Despite Angelina's nagging, he had stopped answering the phone and refused to return messages.

For a second, this realization made him sad. Then he noticed Carla's eyes and, like the other night over pizza, her eyes were laughing. They hinted that she knew the punch line to some secret joke. They were crinkly, forty-something-year-old eyes, but they were dark and mischievous, and in that moment all he

wanted was to understand the joke.

ELEVEN

At first, Delroy tried to hide his association with the Barkers from Lucille, but Freddie had taken a shine to him. He was always sending his girl, Paula, over with plates of Ma's home cooking. Being an Okie, she mostly made corn fritters, and they usually tasted awful. Lucille would take them straight to the trash, wash the plate, and return it after dinner with a big smile. Delroy could hear her in the hall. "Those were surely some tasty fritters, Ma. My own mother couldn't make any better." Ma Barker would giggle as she took the plate, and Lucille would scurry back across the hall. "That damn woman is loony," she'd say, after the door was closed behind her. "She's put together like an ice box with curly hair, and she laughs like a schoolgirl."

Delroy used the money from the Vandalia job to pay Mrs. Finch the rent they owed and buy groceries. Lucille never asked where the money came from, and one night he decided to splurge. Lucille was sitting in her slip, at the table in the kitchenette, mending one of the two dresses she owned, when Delroy plopped a big box down in front of her. "Honey," he said, "I'm fixin' to take you out tonight. Here's a little number I picked up for you to wear." Lucille opened the box and held up its contents, a violet print dress, covered in yellow flowers.

"It's real nice, Dell, but we can't afford new stuff, can we?" She stood up and held it to her chest with one hand while the other played with the hem. "It's kind of low in front, isn't it? Did you pick it out yourself?"

"I don't know anything about dresses. Paula and some of

her friends picked it out for me."

Lucille tossed the dress back in the box. "Them girls are whores," she snapped. "I can't wear it."

Delroy sank into a kitchen chair. "I just wanted to give you something nice. I know you're worried about money and all, but I thought a night on the town might cheer you up. Can't you just wear the damn thing tonight?" He picked a needle out of the pincushion on the table and balanced it crossways on his thumb. "If you don't spill anything on it we can take it back tomorrow. We'll tell 'em you've already got one like it."

They took the streetcar to the Loop and got off at Madison. It was a hot summer evening, but the streets were filled with people. It seemed anyone who wasn't at the World's Fair had come into the Loop. They strolled over to State Street and joined the crowd walking south along the sidewalk, stopping to watch a hawker demonstrating fountain pens. Delroy was mesmerized by the fast-talking salesman. He had just about made up his mind to buy a pen when Lucille whispered in his ear, "Look at his shirt cuffs." The man's right cuff was covered with blue stains—the pen leaked. They moved on past clothing stores and street vendors, crossing the cobbled street and merging with the throng, admiring the array of colorful summer dresses and handsome suits. Delroy was hot but kept his jacket and hat on. Lucille was surprised to see so many men wearing skimmers; she thought the straw hat had passed out of style.

They got to the Orpheum too late for the vaudeville; Harrison and Fisher had just finished performing, but they were in time for a newsreel and the feature, *She Done Him Wrong*, starring Mae West. Afterwards, they ate at The Berghoff, the first place in Chicago to get a liquor license after repeal. Women weren't allowed at the stand-up bar, so they dined at a table. A stuffy

German waiter brought them beer and shrimp cocktails. As he walked to the kitchen Lucille made faces at him behind his back. Delroy was the happiest he'd been in a long time. He reached across the table for Lucille's hand.

"Look at this place," he said. "They've got tablecloths and everything."

Lucille put her beer down, wiped some foam from her lip, and took Delroy's outstretched hand. "It's fancy all right, but that waiter is awful snooty. He gives me a pain."

"Don't worry about him," Delroy said. "He just don't know how stupid he looks with that apron wrapped around his waist."

On the ride home they sat, smiling and tired, in the half-empty streetcar with their arms around each other. Delroy kept sniffing her hair until, finally, Lucille craned her head around so she could look into his eyes. She drawled, à la Mae West, "Hello there, warm, dark, and handsome. Why don't you come up sometime and see me?"

Delroy glanced around the streetcar and, when he thought no one was looking, slid his hand in the front of the violet dress. Lucille's nipples were hard, and Delroy bent to kiss her. They stayed that way until they heard a cough from a dark corner at the back of the car. Then they jumped off and walked the rest of the way home, holding hands and laughing.

The St. Paul Post Office job didn't go quite as smoothly as the Vandalia bank job. In addition to Delroy, there was Freddie, Karpis, Monty Bolton, and an older guy, Chuck Fitzgerald. George Zeigler was in Reno laundering the money from the Hamm kidnapping. Delroy had discovered that, despite their constant bickering, Bolton and Zeigler were good friends who'd worked together since 1929 when they'd helped Al Capone out with one of his little problems in a garage on Clark Street.

Fitzgerald didn't like having Delroy along and complained the whole way to St. Paul about having to work with "amateurs." Another of his complaints was that Delroy would get a percentage of the take instead of a flat fee.

"Even the best lookout is only worth five Cs, tops," he griped. "This hillbilly is takin' the bread outa my mouth, and he'll prolly screw up and get us all killed to boot."

Delroy didn't know whether to tell him off or keep hush. He didn't know Fitzgerald and he didn't trust him not to pull out a gun at the least insult. Freddie intervened.

"Watch that 'hillbilly' stuff," he said. "Me and Ma are country folk, too, and I'd as soon have one like Dell here than five city-bred sharpies."

Not only was the take bigger on this job, but the setup was more complicated. The target was a payroll shipment that was being transferred from the post office to a bank a few blocks away. The complication was that the cops were to escort the bank messengers up the street in two patrol cars.

They'd cased the post office the day before and, as they passed through the lobby, Delroy stopped to look at a half-finished mural, high up on the wall over the counter. Large, square-jawed men were frozen in poses depicting various types of physical labor. Pioneer farmers were cutting down trees and straining behind plows. Shirtless factory workers poured molten steel and welded ship hulls, the sparks tinting their muscles with blue highlights. Not one of the figures was skulking in a doorway, keeping an eye out for the cops. It was a tribute to honest work, and Delroy felt shamed by it. He stood with his hands in his pockets, staring up at it. Freddie had to shove him to get him moving.

Now he was positioned at the second floor hall window of a hotel across the street, his eyes focused on the front door of the post office. The tropical print window curtains had been faded by the sun and darkened by grime from the busy street below. There was a layer of dirt on the sill, too, and the stink of urine drifted up to Delroy from the nearby staircase. He was miserable.

The cops had left their cars at the curb and gone inside to get the messengers. When they emerged with the money Delroy stuck a big National Recovery Act sticker in the middle of the window and crouched down, peering over the sill at the spectacle below.

The black Auburn sedan roared around the corner with Karpis at the wheel and stopped, nose out, in front of the lead cop car. Freddie jumped out of the car first, but he was nervous and came out shooting. He was using a Thompson with a 50-round drum, and he sprayed everything in view. He disabled the lead car and cut down one of the messengers but, when the cops started returning his fire, he had to duck back behind the Auburn. Karpis was firing his pistol from inside the car and had one of the cops pinned down. The remaining patrol car tried to pull around them, but Freddie sent a burst its way and it hurtled out of control, bounced up a curb and came to rest on the sidewalk. Fitzgerald and Bolton used shotguns to convince the remaining bank messengers to drop the money sacks. One of them turned to run and Fitzgerald blew his legs out from under him.

Delroy turned his back to the window and slumped down onto the floor. He pulled the square-headed nail from his Kentucky farmhouse out of his pocket and looked at its rust-pitted surface. He ran his thumb along the tapered edge, then closed his hand over it and squeezed until the point bit into his flesh.

"What have I come to?" he sobbed. He hooked his elbow over the sill, pulled himself to his feet and raced down the stairs. He intended to run off. Leave the gang there. Somehow get back to Chicago, grab Lucille, and hightail it to Kentucky. When he got to the street though, he saw Fitzgerald, bloody, on the ground, dragging himself toward the already moving car. He pulled him into the sedan while Freddie blasted away at cars, cops, anything that moved, including a streetcar that had been unlucky enough to enter the battlefield. Then Freddie and Bolton jumped in after them. The Auburn was fast for its size. Karpis hit the gas, and they were away.

TWELVE

Gilbert purposely accelerated and braked too fast on the drive to Busse Woods from Oak Park. He wanted to shake up his passenger. The funeral home was only a few blocks from the Eisenhower Expressway, but from there it was twenty-five miles out to the forest preserve. Gilbert turned up the radio to drown out the yelling from the trunk as he sped west.

Even on a weekday there were people in the picnic area but Gilbert had scouted out a spot the day before. He drove past the public areas to one of the maintenance roads that led back into the woods. There was a chain across the road to prevent unauthorized access, but Gilbert had previously cleared away a pile of fallen branches to the left of the entrance. He maneuvered the Taurus through the trees and drove down the road to a small clearing where he turned the car around and parked. There was no longer any noise coming from the trunk. He doubted that Roger had suffocated, but he couldn't rule out something like a heart attack. After all, the guy wasn't exactly slim.

Gilbert walked up the road to the next bend to make certain he was alone. He could see the little lake through the trees on one side of the road. The afternoon sun filtered through the canopy and dappled the ground around him. The only sounds were the breeze and an occasional warble or chirp. If he held perfectly still he could just pick up shouts from a soccer game in the picnic area. Gilbert breathed deep. It was a beautiful day, and he had the key to four million dollars in his trunk. He went back to the car, stuck his hand in through the open window, and released the trunk latch. As he reached to lift the lid there was a loud bang and something flew past Gilbert's ear. He threw himself to the ground, rolled to the side of the car, and then sprinted behind a tree. When he peeked out he saw Roger sitting cross-legged in the trunk, holding a gun in one hand and rubbing his eyes with the other.

"I've got a gun!" he shouted. "I'll kill you, you sonuva bitch!"

Gilbert pulled his head back and leaned against the tree. He didn't know whether to laugh or cry. Roger had fired the gun from inside the trunk and obviously deafened himself. Sitting in the trunk, in his shiny suit, and blinking against the sunlight, he looked like a little blue bird with a hangover. Gilbert had to do something quickly, before some nosy picnicker heard Roger's shooting and yelling. He didn't want to shoot back. He didn't want to mess up his car or his chance of finding the gold coins. There was a broken branch at his feet, and he quietly bent and picked it up along with a fist-sized rock. Roger had fired blind. He couldn't know where Gilbert was hiding. He bent low and took another peek. Roger was still rubbing his eyes. Gilbert stepped out from behind the tree and threw the rock into the woods on the far side of the car. Roger looked in the direction of the noise and, when he did, Gilbert stepped out and splintered the branch on the back of his head. Roger slumped forward, and Gilbert reached around and plucked the gun from his hand.

"Oldest trick in the book," he chuckled. He pocketed the gun and pulled Roger up to a sitting position. He was moaning and holding his head but he was still conscious. Gilbert grabbed him under the arms and dragged him over the lip of the trunk.

"Stand up here, tough guy. You and me are taking another

---

little walk." He pulled an old extension cord out of the trunk and shoved Roger toward the woods. He had to use both hands to keep him upright as he steered him through the trees to a little clearing. He pushed Roger down to sit on a fallen log, then used the cord to bind his hands and feet.

"What do you want from me?" Roger asked. "I don't even know you." He tried to wipe away the tears that had started streaming down his cheeks, but the cord was too short. He bent forward and wiped his face on his sleeve. Gilbert bent down and collected a handful of pebbles and small sticks. He stood in front of Roger and started tossing them at him, one by one, aiming for the other man's bulbous nose.

"You and I have something in common," Gilbert said. "We both want your mother's money."

Roger tried to pull his hands up to protect his eyes but only succeeded in yanking his feet off the ground. He struggled to keep his balance, then ducked his head and sat bent over, the pebbles bouncing off his balding scalp. He clenched his fists and shouted at the ground.

"You mean that lousy six thousand I got? There was supposed to be forty thousand dollars! She told me she had set it aside for me in a separate account. I had plans for that money." His voice got softer, and he sat up, blinking at a stick that bounced off his forehead. Gilbert watched his face go slack as all the energy drained out of him. His voice dropped to a whimper. "The nursing home and the doctors got most of her money, but she promised me forty thousand, and there was only six."

Gilbert dropped his pebbles and wiped the dirt from his hands on Roger's shoulder. "Your mother," he said, "may have known where four million dollars in gold was buried. I'll tell you what. I'm gonna let you in on it. We'll be partners. All you have to do is tell me about your mother's first husband, Fred Goetz."

"She couldn't have known anything about any gold. We struggled to get by all our lives. The forty thousand I was supposed to get was the rest of my father's insurance money. Anyway, she never talked about her first husband."

Gilbert propped one foot on the log and looked down at him. "Just think for a minute, Roger. She may have said something that didn't mean anything to you at the time but could help us now. What about her friends? Did she ever talk about people she knew before she married your father?"

"No, we weren't close. We didn't really talk much after she went into the home. She kind of blamed me for putting her there."

"What about her belongings? Maybe she left a diary or some letters or a photo album or something."

Roger winced. "Peg, my wife, and I threw all that stuff out when she went into the home. That's another reason she wouldn't talk to me. Really, I thought it was just a lot of junk. She never had anything that was worth anything."

Gilbert was getting frustrated. "You put your mother in a nursing home and got rid of all her possessions and you're surprised she was mad at you? What are you, an idiot?"

"You don't know what it was like." Roger started sobbing. "She was very demanding. Peg said she'd leave me if my mother continued to live with us. They hated each other." He looked at Gilbert. "What was I supposed to do?"

Gilbert put his hands in his pockets and began to pace back and forth. He looked at the pathetic creature sitting hunched over on the log. Tears had painted streaks in the dirt on his face. The silly shit had screwed himself out of his inheritance and, at the same time, screwed Gilbert out of four million dollars.

He was a washout. They both were. Gilbert felt Roger's gun in his pocket. He pulled it out. It was a hammerless .38 Special with a two-inch barrel. He waved it at Roger. "Why are you carrying this around?"

"I always carry a piece, for self-protection. You know, just in case. At home I keep a 9mm next to the bed but it made too big a bulge in my suit, so I got the little .38."

"What are you, one of those gun nuts?"

"Hey!" Roger bristled. "If everyone was carrying, the criminals wouldn't have the balls to try anything. Hell, I'd like to see one of them try something with me."

Gilbert laughed. "Yeah. You'd show 'em. You're lucky you didn't blow your own head off when you tried to shoot me." He spun the gun on his finger like a movie cowboy. "What? Did you read an article in some gun magazine? I'll bet you practice your fast draw and your menacing scowl in front of the mirror."

Roger looked down at his feet. "Don't," he said. "You. Peg. My mother. Everyone thinks I'm a loser."

"You lost me four million dollars," Gilbert said. He put the gun to Roger's temple and pulled the trigger. The shot was louder than he expected and it startled him. He took out his knife and cut the extension cord from Roger's wrists and ankles. He put the gun in Roger's hand and closed his fingers over the grip. "If they check your hand for gunshot residue, they'll find it. You fired that gun earlier, remember?" He picked up the cord and headed back to his car. At the spot where the chain crossed the road Gilbert got out and walked back to the clearing, dragging a pine branch along to obscure his tire tracks. "Poor guy must have taken a cab to the forest preserve and then walked to the clearing to blow his brains out.

No tellin' what a devoted, grief-stricken son will do."

THIRTEEN

An opening at a Michigan Avenue art gallery wasn't the sort of event that McKinney was used to frequenting, and he was impressed that one of Carla's sculptures was being exhibited at a snooty place like the Halston. He was happy to be on his second date with her in less than a week. On their first date her charm had won over the regulars at the Cermak Lounge. All the old bluesmen had flocked around her. Reverend Emmett pulled up a bar stool and sat with them the entire evening and a guitar player called Mumbles had talked to her for twenty minutes straight. McKinney couldn't understand a word the man said but Carla claimed they had a "lovely conversation." Even the club's owner, a crusty, old hippie-type named Kenny, took a shine to her. "You oughta hang on to this one, McKinney," he'd growled. "It's the first time in months I've seen you smile."

Tonight they were hobnobbing at the other end of the social scale, not that McKinney minded. He liked Carla and was pleased to be invited. Besides, it was a good way to get his mind off work. He had moved on from the Drenon and Burdett cases, but he was still convinced that the two were related; the shoeprints indicated that. What did those two people have in common? And the big question: why were they tortured and killed? He hadn't heard any more from Detective Boadu, and he was relieved. He was glad to be out of it.

The gallery space was a large fourth-floor room with framed art hung on a couple of freestanding walls and sculptures displayed on blocky white pedestals. The wall closest to Michigan Avenue was solid glass, an enormous window that offered an unrestricted view of the Magnificent Mile from the Old Water Tower almost to the river. McKinney looked out on the last of the shoppers heading home with their bags from Tiffany and Nieman Marcus. Carla was across the room, standing in front of a big, lime green painting, drinking red wine and talking with some of the other artists represented in the show. McKinney decided to wander, going from piece to piece, taking them in—miniature oil paintings, life-size nudes, an installation made of one thousand jelly jars. He stopped to study Carla's sculpture. She primarily worked with metal and had jewelry for sale at several boutiques around the city, but this piece was something special, a foot-tall statue of a little girl playing in the rain. It had been cast in bronze from her original clay sculpture, and both the mold and the original had broken during production. It was the only one that would ever be made and it was priced at eight thousand dollars. As he studied the piece McKinney called on his ability to be an objective observer; he didn't want whatever feelings he had for Carla to prejudice his opinion of her work. He moved back, then came in close. He ran his fingertips across the cool, smooth metal.

The girl was about five or six years old and she was splashing through a puddle. Her wet face was turned up to the sky, eyes closed, grateful smile. The folds of her dress accentuated the motion of her kicking leg. Detail had been sacrificed for mood. It was an Impressionist statue. McKinney decided that he liked it, but he still couldn't be sure how much he was influenced by knowing the artist, or by having a daughter whom he'd seen playing in the rain. One thing was certain—the statue evoked feelings in him that shattered his efforts to remain objective. Any woman who had the ability to capture a child's exuberance in a lump of metal was worth getting to know better.

He continued his trek around the room, examining one

piece after another, finally stopping in front of a painting of a black cat. The cat was curled in a ball, sleeping on a wooden floor next to a rocking chair. A heavyset man wearing a dark blue Armani suit with an orange and green striped tie walked up next to him and gestured toward the painting. A few drops of martini sloshed out of the glass in his hand, narrowly missing the canvas.

"Whadaya think?" he asked.

"I like this one," McKinney said. "It's deceptive. At first glance it just looks like a painting of a cat, but look…" he said, pointing, "the cat's tail is under one of the rockers. You can't see whether or not anyone is sitting in the chair but, if someone is and they lean back, the rocker will catch the cat's tail. There's some implied tension there."

The white-haired man snorted. "Hell," he said. "It's a paintin' of a freakin' cat." He drained his glass, turned and lurched off toward the bar. McKinney moved on to a six-foot square canvas of solid blue with a small, red dot in the lower, right-hand corner. He squinted to read the title, "Blue #2." He didn't think much of it and was about to walk away when Carla walked up behind him and linked her arm through his.

"Do you know who that was you were talking to?" she asked.

"Yeah, some guy whose necktie would make a moth vomit."

"That's Bryan O'Boyle. He's a big shot in Chicago politics. The word on the street is that he could be the next mayor."

"You mean 'da' next mayor."

Carla gestured toward the large, blue painting. "Do you like it?"

"It's okay in this space," he said. "But I wouldn't want it hanging in my living room."

"Do you get what the artist is saying?"

"I don't know…he likes blue?"

She snickered. "Okay, but he's also pointing out how even a little bit of one color changes the way we perceive another color. It's more effective if you consider all three of his 'Blue' paintings together. One has a spot of white, which really makes the blue appear lighter. The other has a spot of yellow, which gives the painting a greenish quality."

"That is kind of interesting," he agreed. "But it's not thirteen thousand dollars' worth of interesting. Some of these paintings just seem like artists' conceits."

"Like what?"

He pointed to a large canvas covered with colorful, squiggly lines and blobs. "Well, I don't want to sound like one of those jerks who looks at an abstract expressionist painting and says 'my kid can paint better than that' but it seems like that was probably more fun for the artist to paint than for us to look at."

"What do you mean?"

"Well, it's like someone playing 'Purple Haze' on the Sousaphone. They're probably having a fine time doing it, but I'd rather not have to listen. Do you want to know what I think of your sculpture?"

"Jeez, I don't know, Sean. Think I can take it?"

He grinned at her. "I think you've managed to express joy and innocence in a way that people can understand. You've made art that touches people. I agree that there's room for art that makes people think, but making them feel? That's quite an accomplishment."

After the opening, they walked a few streets west to a Mexican restaurant on Clark Street to celebrate. The River North area was between crowds. The shoppers and tourists had gone home and it was still too early for the nightclub goers. As they walked they could hear the tap-tap of their shoes on the pavement, echoing off the buildings. Streetlights cast long shadows and drained everything else of color. McKinney was reminded of how magical the city could look at night. He stopped and pulled Carla into an empty doorway, put his back against the cool brick wall and leaned to kiss her. She pulled him into a kiss that tasted like wine. He heard other pedestrians giggle as they passed the doorway, but he kept kissing her, and he was pleased that she was undeterred as well. After several minutes they stopped to breathe. "If I had eight thousand dollars I'd buy your statue," he said.

Carla smiled. "You're just saying that because you're horny."

"Horny or not, it's nice."

"I'm not sure I'd let you buy one of my pieces. I think I'd feel funny about it. You know. Maybe some day I'll give you a sculpture, as a gift."

He kissed her again. "I'll look forward to it."

The restaurant was a welcome contrast to the sparse décor of the art gallery. The walls were arrayed with a variety of colors and shapes and there were several paintings by well-known Mexican muralists. They sat at a chunky pine table, painted sky blue and lit by a tin-shaded ceiling lamp. McKinney ordered tilapia that had been steamed in a banana leaf with herbs and spices. He recognized the chili and cilantro but there was one subtle flavor he couldn't identify. He gave Carla a taste.

"That's epazoté," she said. "My mother used to cook with it all the time. It's popular in Mexican cooking."

"So how's your Spanish? I haven't noticed an accent, except when you ordered your dinner. Nice 'R' rolling, babe."

"I grew up in the Logan Square neighborhood, so I heard

Spanish on the street every day while I was a kid. Plus, my parents spoke it at home, but after we started school they really pushed my brother and me to use English. I can still make myself understood most of the time, though."

"Well, I love the way it sounds. Angelina's mother spoke a little bit of Italian. It came in handy on our one trip to Florence. I had two years of French in college, of which I remember *rien*."

"I guess you really miss your wife. Angelina talks about her all the time."

"Yeah, well…" He pushed a pile of rice around his plate with a fork. The conversation was heading into dangerous territory. "I didn't know you and Angelina were such good friends. How did I miss out on that little detail?"

"Really? Maybe there are other things you don't know about your daughter. Do you know she writes poetry?"

"Actually, I do know that. She started writing shortly after Catherine died. She let me read a couple of them. One was about springtime being difficult for her, all the blossoming flowers reminding her that her mother wasn't coming back. Sadly, it was around that time she lost her interest in entomology. She and I used to go bug hunting together when she was little. She wanted to learn all about them. I guess that was one of the casualties of Catherine's death, too."

"Did you know that she has a boyfriend?"

"Yeah, Richard, I think. Skinny kid with curly hair, looks like a giant Q-Tip."

"Richard was two boys ago. This one is Jaime. He's a senior. I'm only telling you this because I think it's important that you know. Please don't tell her I told you."

"No problem. I guess I haven't exactly been an involved parent lately."

"You know she worries about you, don't you?"

"She thinks I cut myself off from people after Catherine died."

"Well, you're not exactly the most gregarious neighbor. I bet you don't even know about our garden club. Mrs. Vladic and Vishal and I all share a space out by the garage. We usually meet out there on Sunday afternoons to weed and water and drink beer. Angelina started coming out to chat with us a couple of months ago. We gave her a few plants of her own to tend and now she's a regular. It's a nice way for us to have a little connection with nature, even though we live in the city."

"Hmmm. I know Mrs. Vladic but who's Vishal?"

"That's the East Indian gentleman who lives on the first floor. He owns a fabric store up on Devon. He moved in over a year ago, Sean."

"Ohhh, sure, I've seen him getting his mail."

"Nice. Listen, I don't want to pry. I mean, I know this can be a sensitive subject, but if you ever want to talk to someone about your wife…"

McKinney looked away. He was uncomfortable talking about Catherine, especially with someone he had recently kissed. It wasn't so much that he felt unfaithful—he did—but he knew that would pass. Catherine's death had been quite a learning experience. It had shown him something about himself that disgusted him. He couldn't tell Carla about it and he certainly could never tell Angelina.

"Thanks. I appreciate that, and just so you know, I'm not trying to replace her."

Carla's hand froze on its way to her wine glass and her head snapped up, pushing her chin toward McKinney so quickly that he sat back in his chair. "Look, I like you and we've had some fun together but I'm not applying for a job here."

McKinney held both hands up, palms facing her. "Whoa, I think maybe you misunderstood what I was trying to say." He reached to take her still outstretched hand but she drew it back. "I just don't want you to feel pressured or think I'm shopping for a mother for Angelina. That's all I meant."

"Maybe it's too soon for you. I had this same problem with a divorced guy I dated. The last thing I need is someone who can't figure out whether he's 'emotionally available' or not," she said, making air quotes with her fingers.

McKinney looked down at the mangled mess on his plate. *Damn*, he thought, *why's she making such a big deal out of this? Maybe she's the one who's emotionally unavailable.*

"Come on, Carla. It's not like that."

"Maybe it is and maybe it isn't, but I don't know if I have the patience to find out." She fished a twenty-dollar bill out of her purse and laid it on the table. "I'll take a cab. Good night, Sean."

She was up and moving before McKinney could stop her. He tossed more money on the table and rushed to follow her out. A group of giggling young women pushed past him and, by the time he made the sidewalk, Carla was getting into a taxi. As the cabbie drove away she looked out of the back window at him.

The night air had turned cool, and he slipped his sport coat on. As he did his cell phone rang. It played a few bars of "Sweet Home Chicago" before he got it out of his pocket. He recognized Nina Anderson's voice right away. He hadn't thought of her in days.

"I'm sorry to bother you outside of office hours but I have to go back into court with Phillips on Monday morning, and I haven't heard anything from Dave Barger yet. I was hoping you'd talked to him."

"I haven't," McKinney said. "I spoke with the investigator on the other case I was telling you about, the Burdett murder. He said he'd call Detective Barger and ask him to take another look at Mr. Drenon's case, maybe reopen it."

"Did he? I mean, did he reopen it?"

"I don't know. Neither of them has contacted me."

"Well, you're just about my whole case then, McKinney. I can present Phillips's medical records and history, but that's not going to convince the jury he didn't do it. In fact, people who don't understand autism might think his mental illness explains his missing motive."

"Or that he was getting revenge for being sent to an institution as a child."

"I'd thought of that, too," she said. "I'm sure Jameson will play up that angle. I just wish Barger wasn't so stubborn. He still won't return my calls. I probably won't need you to testify on Monday. We'll be doing jury selection all day. I'll probably put you on the stand later in the week."

"Well, just let me know. Send a subpoena to the lab, too. Standard procedure."

He and Carla had taken the El downtown; parking in the River North area was expensive and hard to find. McKinney played with the wedding ring in his pocket as he trudged back to the station. Lightning momentarily illuminated the street and the brick walls that towered over him on either side. He heard a crack of thunder, then the sky opened up. He was soaked before he reached the platform. On the train he stood, dripping in the aisle and shivering, as it clackety-clacked him north to Wrigleyville.

FOURTEEN

Delroy hadn't seen the Barkers in several weeks and that was fine with him. He was determined not to have anything more to do with killing and robbing. This was his twelfth day of beating his gunboats on the pavement, going door to door, looking for work. It was only mid-morning but it was warm for October, and he'd been out since six. He was tired. Today his walk had taken him over to Harrison and Canal, almost to the train yards. He picked up a discarded *Tribune* and was scanning the ads as he walked, so he didn't notice the limping man until he was almost on top of him. Even then, he might not have looked up from his paper except for the smell. The man's body odor took hold of Delroy's nose and snapped his head up.

Shuffling toward him, shifting his weight from his good leg to his crutch and back again, was a man who appeared to be made from scraps of material. His coat and pants were patched with rags, some sewn on, but most knotted together and hanging loose. Delroy could see that they had once been all different shapes and colors, but several layers of dirt made it impossible to tell where one rag ended and another picked up. He couldn't tell whether the man was fat or thin under the rags as the whole mess billowed out around him. As soon as he had Delroy's attention he stuck out his free hand and smiled. His half a dozen teeth shone out white from the grimy pallor of his face. Without thinking, Delroy shook the man's hand.

"How 'bout stakin' me to some breakfast, brother," the raggedy man said. "I just rode the Illinois Central in last night, and I ain't et nothin' since Effingham."

"I can't do it," Delroy said. "I'm about busted, myself. I'm out lookin' for work right now." Delroy tried to take his hand back, but the man had a strong grip and wasn't interested in letting go.

"Lookin' for work, huh? I hope that's not contagious. Listen, what say you and me head over to the jungle. Like as not someone'll have some coffee on, and there's a fella what comes by every day, lookin' for workers. Some kinda jobber, I guess." The man finally let go of Delroy's hand and, putting his free hand on Delroy's shoulder, spun on his crutch and limped off, dragging Delroy along with him. Delroy pulled away and stopped on the sidewalk. He took out his handkerchief and wiped his eyes. The man's smell was making them water. "What jungle?" he asked.

"Hobo jungle," the man said, as he pointed around the corner. "There."

Delroy stepped forward and looked. Across Canal Street was an open field filled with tents and packing crates and a few slapped together huts. Smoke drifted up from a dozen fires. Hundreds of men sat or stood around the fires, talking, eating, shaving, and drinking. Delroy could make out a few dogs, roaming the camp, begging for scraps. "This is where you live?" he asked.

"When I'm in town. They call me Birmingham, but I ain't been south in a couple years." He headed off across the street and Delroy went with him.

The jungle was crowded and, as they passed among the men, Delroy noticed that they all seemed to have a "hey" or a nod for his guide. Someone shouted, "Who's the new blanket stiff, Birmingham?"

"No stiff," the man called back. "Just a citizen." Delroy

saw few women in the ranks of men, and all but a couple were off by themselves. A woman wearing men's trousers and a plaid shirt sat in front of a fire, holding her knees and rocking back and forth, mumbling. Birmingham saw Delroy staring at her. "That's Nell," he said. "She lost her boy last week. Poor kid slipped when they were climbing into an open boxcar and went under the wheels. Now she don't eat or nothin'. Just sits there."

The odor of unwashed bodies and rotting food mingled with the smoke from the cook fires. Delroy started to put his hands over his nose, then stopped and shoved them in his pockets. He didn't want to rub anyone the wrong way. He was nervous but fascinated. He'd read about the shack towns of wandering men that had sprung up around the country. He imagined his brothers must have seen a few of them when they went out west, looking for work. He'd thought hoboing would be kind of fun, an adventure on the open road. These men didn't look like they were having fun. One silent group was decked out with brown-stained bandages. One of them, a man with silver-white hair, held his obviously broken arm in his lap, the forearm above the wrist bulging out at an unnatural angle. Birmingham gestured toward them with his crutch. "Railroad bulls caught 'em. Most just got knocked around a little, but they threw Grady out of a moving boxcar." He paused in front of the group. "How's the arm, Grady?" he asked. The man tried to pick up his arm to show but, as he did, all the color drained out of his face. He sucked air through his gritted teeth, then lay down on his side. As they moved on through the rows of men Delroy could hear him whimper.

They walked deep into the hobo jungle, all the way back to the Chicago River. Finally, Birmingham found the group he was looking for. Half a dozen men, both black and white, sat around a small pile of glowing coals with a coffee pot suspended from a bent piece of iron rod. He let his crutch drop and followed it down to the ground, his ragged clothes settling around him like a pile of leaves. He gestured to an open patch of ground. Delroy sat.

"Hey, Hubert," Birmingham said, "how 'bout fixin' us up with some coffee?"

One of the black men poured a steaming, ochre liquid from the pot into two empty cans and handed them across to the newcomers. "Careful," he said. "They hot."

Delroy sniffed the contents of the can. It smelled like motor oil more than coffee. He didn't want to drink it but he was aware of the men watching him. He took a sip. "Thanks."

"This here citizen is lookin' for work," Birmingham said. "I told him 'bout that fella with the jobs. He been by here yet?"

"Y'all just missed him," Hubert said. "He had a good job today, too. Gonna take men over to where they's tearin' down a building. Give you a hammer and let you chip the old mortar off the bricks. Pay ten cents for ever' hunnerd bricks you clean."

Birmingham winked at Delroy, then turned back to Hubert. "How come you ain't out there workin' right now? Didn't you want no job?"

"Same as yesterday. Cain't use no colored workers."

One of the other black men spit a gob of tobacco juice onto the coals. He watched it sizzle for a second. "I used to be a bricklayer back home," he said. "I'd like to take one of those hammers and smack that white sonuva bitch in the head."

A white man sitting next to him put his hand on the man's shoulder. "Now, Dill," he said, "you don't mean that." Dill shrugged the other man's hand off, stood up, and stalked away.

"That's Dill," Birmingham said. "We call him Dill Pickle.

He and these other boys traveled clear from Detroit down to Virden, Illinois 'cause they heard they could get work in the coal mines."

"Yeah," said Hubert, "but when we got there it turned out the miners was on strike. The mining company was hiring scabs. We tried to go down in the mine, but the strikers attacked us." He leaned forward to show Delroy a wound on his forehead. "I got hit with a pipe. Then the Pinkertons opened fire."

"We hightailed it outta there," said Dill as he made his way back to the circle. "Those Pinks was supposed to protect us from the miners, but they couldn't tell who was who. They shot at everybody. We were lucky to get out with our skins."

"Yeah, lucky," Hubert said. "Only we still ain't got no jobs. We got no money, and that means no dinner."

"Well, I'm goin' back to Michigan," said Dill. "I got a wife and a little boy. They stayin' at my daddy's place. Soon's it gets dark, I'm headin' over to the rail yard."

Delroy took a slow look around the fire at the men's faces. He had never seen a more wretched bunch in his life. He had just about determined to go home, clean out the kitchen cupboard, and bring all the food back for them when Hubert reached across and tugged on his sleeve. "That jobber fella said there was some work at the bus station, loading freight. You might as well go on down there and see. I'm goin' back to Detroit, too. I think we've all had 'bout enough of Illinois."

Delroy shook the man's hand. "Thank you, thank you, thank you." He reached into his pocket and pulled out a crumpled dollar bill, his lunch money. "This is for you fellas. Maybe you can have yourselves a little meal before you go."

Birmingham grabbed the money. It disappeared beneath his rags. "I'll take this. I know where I can get us some ears of corn and some beans."

"Not them pinto beans," Hubert said. "I'm sicka them pintos."

"These are green beans," Birmingham said. "Fresh green beans, right off the farm."

Delroy sprang to his feet. "Thanks again," he called as he ran off, weaving through the tents and the groups of men. He could hear Birmingham describing the delights of fresh green beans all the way to Canal Street.

FIFTEEN

Gilbert Anglin stood on the Galena Boulevard Bridge and looked out at little Stolp Island in the Fox River. A delivery truck rumbled over the bridge, spewing exhaust. Gilbert swore at the driver as it passed. His trip to Aurora wasn't going well and he was frustrated and angry. He had driven out that morning and found the red brick ranch house he believed was Gertrude Billiter's with no trouble, but the nameplate over the bell said Hoskins and there was no response to his repeated ringing and knocking. What if this old broad was dead too? He'd tried the neighbors on either side and across the street, but none of them were home.

The rest of the day had been spent wandering around downtown Aurora. He'd eaten lunch in a little mom and pop restaurant and lingered over coffee and the newspaper. There was a flock of geese swimming around Stolp Island and Gilbert ran his hand over the gun in his pocket as he watched them. His frustration had put him in a murderous mood, and he imagined himself taking aim and plugging goose after goose until the river was awash with blood and feathers.

Instead he drove back to the Hoskins house and rang the bell again. When he was convinced that no one was home he walked around to the back and, using an eight-inch pry bar, popped the lock on the back door and let himself in. Rather than risk turning on the lights, he used his Maglite as he went from room to room. The rooms were small but extremely neat and smelled like roses. The hallway had a plastic runner over the rug and the living room chairs and sofa were encased in plastic.

There were paintings of farm animals on every wall, mostly sheep. On a small table near the front door he found a stack of opened mail addressed to Gertrude Hoskins. Gilbert was relieved. Gertrude was a fairly uncommon name. Hoskins was probably Gertrude Billiter's married name. He flipped through the mail, tossing bills and catalogs on the floor. In addition to the junk mail there were two open letters reminding Gertrude about meetings at her church and a funeral announcement. The funeral was taking place that day up in Waukegan—quite a drive. That would explain why no one had been home all day.

The bedroom was filled with gingham and needlepoint and little ceramic dioramas of barefoot children with titles like *Goin' Fishin'* and *The Old Swimmin' Hole*. Gilbert picked up *Indian Summer* and tossed it across the room. Instead of shattering, it bounced off the thick shag rug with an unsatisfying thump. He kicked it out of the way as he crossed the room to the roll-top desk in the corner. He nosed around in the desk for about twenty minutes, finally coming up with something useful—a diary, a recent birthday card from Gertrude's daughter, and a packet of letters.

He shoved the letters into his coat pocket and sat back to read the diary. It was the kind of diary and date book that was sold in drugstores in the 1940s. The first thing he did was to hold it by the spine and shake it. Several pieces of paper fell out onto his lap. There were a couple of World War II ration coupons, a photograph of a young man in a military uniform with Cpl. Hoskins written on the back in pencil, and a Valentine. The first entry in the diary, dated March 17, 1944, mentioned Harry Campbell as "my first, true love" and went on to describe the hardship of loving a man who was serving a life sentence in Alcatraz. She talked a little about Campbell's partner, Alvin Karpis, and there was a brief mention of another of the gang members, Volney Davis, who Campbell said had turned rat in prison. Gilbert recalled reading that Davis was one of the gangsters on the Bremer kidnapping.

By the diary's sixth page, however, she had fallen for a younger man, Frank Hoskins, who she met at a USO dance. He was shorter than Harry and a little paunchy, but she thought that he looked a bit like Clark Gable in his uniform. The rest of the diary chronicled their courtship and marriage up to the birth of a daughter, Emaline, in 1948. Glued inside the back cover was a poem, one of Shakespeare's sonnets.

> *Shall I compare thee to a summer's day?*
> *Thou art more lovely and more temperate.*
> *Rough winds do shake the darling buds of May,*
> *And summer's lease hath all too short a date.*
> *Sometime too hot the eye of heaven shines,*
> *And often is his gold complexion dimmed,*
> *And every fair from fair sometime declines,*
> *By chance or nature's changing course untrimmed...*

Gilbert could see that the poem continued but the rest of it was missing, the next line obscured by the tear at the bottom of the paper. *Some of these old broads were probably just like the poem*, he thought. They had started out being the "darling buds of May" but they hooked up with the wrong kind of guys. The ones who weren't caught or killed probably tried to have a normal life, but he didn't see how they could. He imagined they just withered away, like a grape that was left on the vine too long, "too hot the eye of heaven shines." He tossed the diary into his bag and was just getting up to leave when he heard a key in the front door lock. He walked softly to the bedroom door and listened for a minute. Gertrude was home.

"Oh, dear, what a mess."

He heard her footsteps shuffling toward him. He stepped

into the hallway. In front of him was a small elderly woman in a beige overcoat and ivory cloche hat. She held a cane in one hand and the spilled mail in the other. When she saw Gilbert she opened her mouth to shout. He grabbed her with his left hand and simultaneously slapped her with his right. Her eyes got large for a moment, then, as she went limp, rolled back into her head. Her cane fell noiselessly to the carpet. Gilbert caught her before she hit the floor and dragged her to the kitchen. He propped her up in a chair at the kitchen table and checked her pulse. Her heart rate was fast but steady. Her breathing sounded funny to him, though. It was erratic.

"Crap! Don't even fucking die on me, lady. I've got too much time invested—" He stopped and listened. There was a noise from the front of the house.

"Mom?"

Fuck! he thought. *Now what?*

"Mom, are you okay?"

He started back toward the bedroom to get his bag but, as he turned, the old lady slid onto the floor, pulling the tablecloth and sugar bowl with her. The house was suddenly filled with noise.

"Mother?"

Gilbert froze. He heard footsteps coming down the hall. He ducked into the pantry. A heavy-set woman in a brown corduroy barn jacket and green plaid pants rushed into the kitchen and knelt beside the old woman on the floor. Gilbert stepped out of the pantry and shoved the little Beretta in her face. When she screamed he smacked her with his free hand. She fell back on the linoleum and lay there with her nose bleeding, staring up at him. Her eyes were open so wide you could see the whites clear around the iris.

"No noise," he said. "No noise and no hysterics. Now, help

me get the old lady into one of these chairs." He smiled. "Or I'll kill you."

Gilbert was careful to tie the younger of the two women securely. He couldn't tell how much younger she was because her hair was an unnatural shade of red. A color, he thought, that didn't exist in nature. He lashed her ankles to the front legs of the chair with electrical cords he cut from the microwave and toaster.

"I'm going to ask you some questions," he said, "and I want you to think hard about your answers. Accuracy is very important."

"What did you do to my mother?"

Gilbert smacked her with his open hand again. "You're going to get an awful headache if you don't get with the game plan. I'm going to ask you questions. You are only allowed to speak to tell me what I want to know. If you say anything else, I'll hit you, and if you refuse to answer I'll kill both you *and* your mother."

The woman turned out to be pretty good at Gilbert's game. She whimpered a little, and one eye had started to puff up, but she sat straight and paid attention. She answered his questions without hesitation. She didn't, however, know anything about gangsters or gold. Gilbert took out the packet of letters he'd found in the roll-top desk and began to go through them, one by one, asking her questions about the letters' authors as he went. Finally, he came to the last letter in the bundle. The return address was a nursing home near St. Paul, Minnesota and the letter was signed "Viola Nordquist," a name he recalled from his research. Viola Nordquist had been the girlfriend of Jack Peifer, a Barker/Karpis associate and a big shot in the St. Paul underworld.

"I've never been to St. Paul," she said, "and I don't know

the woman who wrote that letter. Listen, please, you've got to help my mother, her breathing doesn't sound right to me."

Gilbert slapped her again and sat down at the table. A casual observer might have thought they were a family sitting down to a meal together in grandma's kitchen. He looked around the room. It was a stark contrast to any kitchen he'd ever known. The daffodil-colored walls were covered with little plaques and pictures, and a collection of pots and pans hung over the stove. He was surprised to see a cat's food dish on the floor next to the stove because he hadn't seen or smelled a cat. The counters were packed with blenders and mixers and other cooking tools, and everything was shiny and clean. Kitchen counters when he was a kid had always been covered with cigarette burns and coffee cup rings and not much else. This kitchen was neat and tidy. It looked like the kitchens he'd seen on TV. He respected it. The messiest thing in the room was the refrigerator. It was almost hidden by the dozens of photographs that were stuck to it with magnets shaped like cats. Gilbert looked closely. Every one of the cats was black and white. He imagined the people in the pictures were staring out at him, judging him. *Fuck them,* he thought. *What the hell did they know about anything?* Years before, he'd thrown away the only photograph he had of his father. He'd never owned a picture of his mother.

Finally, he turned his attention to Gertrude. She was slumped over, her head hanging forward and her chin resting on her chest, just above the first loop of the cord that held her to the chair. He listened to her breathing over the whimpering of the other woman; it was wheezy but rhythmic. After a moment Gilbert recognized the sound as snoring. Gertrude was asleep. He touched her shoulder and shook her, gently.

"Gertrude," he crooned, "time to wake up. Come on, honey, wake up, and watch me hurt your daughter."

SIXTEEN

McKinney stood at his kitchen window, sipping coffee from a mug with "$C_8H_{10}N_4O_2$," the molecular formula for caffeine, printed on it. Unlike the rest of the apartment, the kitchen walls weren't decorated with Lucite-encased insects. Angelina wouldn't allow it. Instead, there was a poster covered with pictures of pies and cakes—"Periodic Table of the Desserts." Down in the yard, Carla, on her hands and knees, crawled up and down the rows of vegetables. "Probably killing off every beetle she finds," McKinney muttered. He slid in between the window and the kitchen table to get a better view, wishing she'd look at him with her dark, playful eyes again. The thought depressed him. It seemed like he hadn't minded his loneliness quite so much before. It had taken almost two years to get used to it but, once he did, it was kind of a solace. There's a safety in loneliness, McKinney thought, that's comforting, no pressure to be anything other than what you are. If you spill soup on your shirt, or blow your nose on your napkin, nobody will look at you disapprovingly. There's no one for whom you're a diminished expectation, no one to disappoint.

He looked up at the summer sky and saw a single cloud, meandering its way to the horizon, painted gold by the late afternoon sun. He envied it. That kind of loneliness seemed almost attractive. Certainly it was bearable. He lowered his gaze, and there was Carla, looking up in his direction. He jumped back from the window, stepped in the dog's food bowl, and slammed his hip into the table. The sugar bowl rolled to the opposite edge of the table and, before he could catch it, plunged to the floor. He was kneeling on the tile, cleaning up sugar, kibble, and glass, when Angelina came in, holding their gym bags.

"Time for tai chi, Dad. Let's go."

With Carla avoiding him, it seemed like tai chi class was the only time McKinney was able to concentrate on something else, without the Phillips case trespassing on his thoughts. It was like putting his car on cruise control; years of training came into play as he focused his attention. Tonight he was doing some light sparring with one of the senior students. On the other side of the school, Angelina was practicing forms with the rest of the class in front of a mirror that covered all of one wall. The school had been an auto repair shop in a previous incarnation, so there was plenty of floor space. The high ceilings, exposed brick walls, and skylights were atmospheric but made the school expensive to heat or cool, consequently there was no air conditioning. McKinney's shirt was plastered to his back with sweat.

Master Kuo, the instructor, was about McKinney's age but several inches shorter and believed that tai chi should be taught as a martial art, not just as an exercise. He was fond of telling his students, "If you just want to learn to dance, why not take dancing lessons?" Instead of a traditional tai chi uniform he wore track pants and a sweatshirt. He'd been a top competitor in China, and an instructor and coach of the Hubei Province professional martial arts team before moving to the United States. Now, he wandered up and down the long room, correcting postures and giving advice to the eighteen students. He grabbed McKinney's arm and shook it. "Loosen up. You're too tight. You need *peng jin*, expanding energy, not stiffness. Pretend that you are a balloon and the inside air is pressing on all sides, trying to get out."

"Yes, sir."

"And lead the movement with your *dan tian*. The energy should move like a chain, from *dan tian*, up through torso, shoulder, arm, forearm, wrist, and palm."

"Yes, sir."

The *dan tian*, McKinney knew, was about two inches below his belly button, a central point for *chi* or energy development and, in most people, the center of gravity. McKinney was conscious of being too stiff, using muscle instead of proper technique to control his opponent. He and the other student stopped sparring to give Master Kuo their attention. The small man pulled up his sleeves, placed one hand on each of their chests and said, "Watch my body." Then he gave a little shake. To McKinney it looked as though Master Kuo barely moved, but he was thrown back two feet and had to struggle to maintain his balance. The other student slammed into the wall four feet behind him. "Watch a wet dog shaking off water," Master Kuo said. "It moves its body parts in sequence, not all at once."

After class McKinney and Angelina stopped at their favorite neighborhood restaurant, the Beau Thai, for dinner. It had a mixed menu of traditional Thai dishes and vegetarian sandwiches. The atmosphere was nineteen seventies coffee house, with paintings and art prints on the walls and an old jukebox filled with jazz and blues records. They were discussing class over spicy *tom ka* soup and *pad see eiw* noodles when McKinney's attention was drawn to a framed print on the wall behind Angelina. It was a reproduction of an Art Nouveau poster, *Clinique Chéron* by Steinlen. The poster was an ad for a veterinary clinic and included drawings of several animals, including a small black cat. He stared at it in silence.

"Dad? Hello?" Angelina waved her hand in front of

McKinney's face. "Where'd you go? You know, you've been acting kind of freaky lately. Is something wrong?"

McKinney looked at his daughter and smiled.

"I think I just figured something out. Did I ever tell you about the cat your mother and I had before you were born?"

"No, I didn't know you guys had any pets before Hendrix."

"You know we named him Hendrix because that was the only musician your mother and I could agree on?"

"Yeah, I know. I heard all his records about a million times when I was little. What about the cat?"

"Well, her name was Kimmy. She was a little calico, a feral cat that hung out in the back yard because your mother fed her all the time. One day your mother decided we should catch her and have her spayed so she wouldn't start cranking out feral kittens. We kept her in a big dog cage in the middle of our little one-bedroom apartment. This was when we lived up in Rogers Park. The neighborhood was kind of run down, but our rent was cheap, and we were only a block from the lake. Anyway, the plan was to let her loose again after the surgery but, by the time she was well enough to be released, it was winter. Your mother was afraid she'd freeze to death."

"So you kept her? I thought Mom was allergic to cats."

"She was. It was horrible. She had headaches and sneezed all the time. We knew we couldn't keep the cat so we decided to give her to a shelter. The problem was that she was still wild. All the time we had her we were never able to touch her. She wanted to be around us and would cry when we left the room, but if you came too close or tried to touch her—yow! You could lose a hand. We decided to try to socialize her so she'd have a better chance of being adopted. We sat on the floor and read to her and sang songs and told her what a pretty cat she was.

Her favorite book was *Fox in Socks* by Doctor Seuss. It's full of tongue twisters. We'd read it together, and when we'd make a mistake your mother would roll on the floor laughing while the cat stared at her like she was crazy." McKinney grinned. "Your mother was good crazy, the kind of crazy that made me want to be around her all the time, just to see what she would do next."

"I remember her reading to me when I was little. She laughed a lot then, too."

"We read *Fox in Socks* to you the same way we read it to the cat."

"What happened to the cat?"

"We found a shelter to take her to right before Christmas, way out in the far south suburbs. Your mother drove three hours to get there but, when she came home, she still had the cat and she was crying. The shelter was full of cute little kittens. That cat didn't have a chance in hell of being adopted, and the man who ran the place told your mother that he would only keep her for a month, and then he'd have to put her down."

"You mean kill her?"

"Yep. She lived with us all winter, and your mother was miserable, but she said, since we had been the ones to start it, we had accepted the responsibility. In the spring we found a farmer who was willing to take her. She went to live as a barn cat, keeping down the mouse population on his farm. After that we moved to the condo in Lincoln Park so we could have baby Angelina."

Angelina looked down at her plate, and when she looked up McKinney realized she was crying. Tears were running down her cheeks so fast she couldn't catch them with her napkin. They were seasoning her soup. She blew her nose. McKinney remembered how, as a little girl, she would refuse to wipe her nose and would squeal whenever Catherine went after her with a tissue. Once Catherine had come home from shopping, full of indignant rage because some "plump pill of a woman," having heard the squeal, had given her a lecture on proper parenting. "If I were a vindictive sort," she'd said, "I would have let Angelina wipe her snotty fingers on the woman's Dior pantsuit."

McKinney reached out to grasp Angelina's free hand. "I miss her, too, honey."

"She was the best mother," Angelina said. "It's just not fair."

Catherine's illness had been hard on all of them. Diagnosed with stage two breast cancer when Angelina was ten years old, she had undergone a full mastectomy, chemo, and radiation. When she lost her hair McKinney had shaved his head in solidarity. Angelina had insisted on shaving her head, too. The act united them as a family, but Angelina suffered at school. The other kids thought she looked "weird." The ones who didn't tease her avoided her. The cancer went into remission for a while, but eventually it returned. Catherine was an unselfish woman who tried to hide her fear from her family, but the last years of her life had been a strange mix of mirth and anxiety. When McKinney thought about it, he was amazed that the same experience that had turned him into an emotional cripple had helped his little girl find some kind of inner strength. He looked at his daughter now and saw the fragility of that strength.

"Do you remember the time she burned the lasagna?" McKinney asked.

"Oh, my God," Angelina snuffled. "That was hysterical."

"The lasagna turned into charcoal, and when she touched it with a spoon it just crumbled to dust. Your mother let out a wail that could be heard clear up in Evanston."

Angelina smiled. "And poor Hendrix hid in the closet to get away from the smoke."

"And what started everyone laughing," McKinney said, "was when you came into the kitchen, oblivious to the billowing smoke and the charred remains, and said, 'What's for dinner? I'm starving.'"

Angelina stopped wiping her eyes. "What made you think about all that?"

"The cat," McKinney said. "I think I finally know why I'm so obsessed with this Phillips case. Somehow, he reminds me of that cat. I know it sounds goofy, but the expression on his face the first time I saw him in court was just like a cornered cat's. He was frightened and vulnerable and didn't really understand what was happening to him. I learned something about responsibility from the way your mother took care of that cat. When I turned over my report to the two attorneys I accepted some kind of responsibility for this guy. I just don't know what to do about it."

The subpoena was for ten a.m., which meant that McKinney probably wouldn't be called to testify until after lunch. The trial was to take place in the same second-floor courtroom at the 26th and California criminal courts building where he had first seen John Phillips. He met Nina Anderson in the marble hallway and they quickly reviewed the questions she would ask him on the stand. He gave her a copy of his curriculum vitae for the initial set of questions that would qualify him as an expert witness, but he knew there would be no problem with that.

Brian Jameson had asked that his qualifications be accepted

at trials in the past, when McKinney was a witness for the prosecution, and he would need him to testify at future trials. He would have to stipulate to McKinney's qualifications. Jameson probably wouldn't even cross-examine him. His most likely move would be to object to McKinney's testimony on the grounds of relevance. It would be up to Anderson to show that McKinney's analysis of the evidence had probative value. Even if Jameson's objections were sustained, the jury would still hear much of what McKinney had to say.

Anderson led him into a small waiting room just outside the courtroom where he could sit and review his notes until it was his turn to take the stand. The room wasn't much bigger than a coat closet, but it contained a rectangular table and several folding chairs. Seated, with his feet on the table, reading a newspaper, was a dark-haired man in a gray three-piece suit. He wore a badge on a lanyard around his neck. The man briefly looked up when McKinney entered, then returned his attention to his newspaper without speaking. McKinney sat at the opposite end of the table and took his notes out of the file folder he carried. Neither man spoke for several minutes. They could hear the muffled buzz from the courtroom as the jury was seated and the attorneys made their opening statements. Finally, the man tossed his newspaper down and took his feet off the table.

"You're McKinney." It was a statement.

"Yep," McKinney said. He held out his hand. "And you're...?"

The man looked at his hand until McKinney drew it back. "Detective Dave Barger. I'm the guy working to keep scum like Phillips off the street so they can't murder old people in their homes. And you're the guy who sent that fat-ass Boadu to get me to reopen the case."

Well, thought McKinney, *at least Detective Boadu kept his promise*. "I'd really like to go over the evidence with you, Detective Barger, but you know we're not allowed to discuss the case before we testify. Maybe later—"

"No thanks, McKinney. We don't have anything to discuss. You'll never catch me working for the defense, especially not this bitch. Not after she got that little girl killed. And, as far as I'm concerned, if you're working for her, you're just as bad as she is."

McKinney tried to control his temper. "What makes you think I'm working for her?"

"Jameson told me. We'll both be having a little talk with your boss."

"Fine," McKinney mumbled. "You do that." He looked down at his papers, hoping the detective was through.

"I saw your report," Barger continued, "and I don't think it outweighs the confession I got out of this slime, and I don't need you or Boadu telling me how to do my job."

McKinney stopped pretending to read. "It's nice to see that you don't allow the facts to interfere with your opinions. Makes your job a lot easier, doesn't it? How did you get that confession? Did you sweat the kid for hours, until he was confused and disoriented? You know he's autistic, don't you? You probably could have gotten him to confess to anything."

"Yeah, I know Phillips has mental problems. I don't know what kind, but I do know what he's taking for it—haloperidol. He had it on him when we picked him up. That's the stuff they give schizos to keep 'em from flipping out. Maybe he forgot to take his medication the day he tortured and killed Mr. Drenon."

"Don't you think—" McKinney started.

A sheriff's deputy opened the door and stuck his head in.

"Quiet down in there," he growled. "We can hear you out in the courtroom."

McKinney whispered, "Don't you think tying up the victim, beating him, and methodically searching his house is a bit too structured for the behavior of someone who's flipping out?"

Barger unfolded his paper and put his feet back on the table. "Screw you, pal."

McKinney took out a pen, wrote "haloperidol" on a scrap of paper and stuck it in his pocket. He'd have to look it up later. *Damn Anderson*, he thought. *Why hadn't she mentioned that? Weren't there any honest lawyers? From now on I'll just do my work and keep my head down.*

A noise from the courtroom interrupted his musing. There were three loud whumps, followed by a crash and a scream. Barger was out of his seat and had the door open when McKinney came up behind him and peered out into the courtroom. Most of the jurors were on their feet, talking and pointing and looking toward the defense table. The judge was banging his gavel, futilely trying to restore order, and deputies were running in from the hallway. Phillips was lying on the floor in the middle of the courtroom, his face covered with blood.

SEVENTEEN

Delroy found Lucille hanging laundry on one of the clotheslines that crisscrossed the little yard behind their rooming house. The sun was shining, and Delroy was happy. He had seen her from the back window when he got home and, in his excitement, climbed down the fire escape to get to her. He grabbed her from behind, spun her to face him and, avoiding the clothespins in her mouth, kissed her forehead.

"I've got big news, honey, big news!"

She took the clothespins out of her mouth and wiped the sheen of sweat from her forehead with the back of her hand, wiping his kiss off with it. "What, you and your friends kill some cops?"

Delroy ignored the jibe. "I've got a job! A real job that pays decent money. I start tomorrow."

"Doin' what?"

"I went down to the hobo jungle, at Harrison and Canal Street, 'cause I heard about a guy who goes there looking to hire day workers. One of the tramps tipped me off about the bus company. They're hiring freight loaders down at the Greyhound. The very same depot we came into from Frankfort. I was so excited I ran almost the whole thirty blocks. I'm gonna be loading and unloading those big dogs and, when there's no freight to pull, they'll put me on the cleaning crew. This ain't day work, honey, it's a real job!"

Lucille sat down on the back steps and covered her face with her apron. The clothespins clattered on the wooden steps as they spilled from the pocket, and her body shuddered with emotion. Finally she wailed. Delroy had never seen her cry like that before, and he didn't know what to do. He reached for her slowly, like he was sticking his hand into a flame, and touched her shoulder. She knocked his hand away and glared up at him, her face wet and angry.

"Thank God," she said. "Thank God, you dumb bastard. I thought I was going to have to take you back to Rockcastle County in a box."

"Aw, come on, now. I know you've been worried, but everything's going to be fine. I was a little worried myself, there. The boys was close to getting caught a couple of times."

"Caught, hell," she said. "I prayed you'd get caught. Every time you went out on a job with those Barkers and that lunatic, Karpis, I prayed. Lord, please don't let him get killed. Let him get caught, or shot in the foot or somethin'. Please don't let him kill anyone. Some poor cop or guard whose wife is probably as scared as I am and whose kids will have to grow up without a daddy."

"I never carried a gun. You know that."

"I only know that I've been scared ever since we left Kentucky, Dell. Not just about you robbin' with those damn Barkers, but about everything. I've been scared every day that we wouldn't have a roof over our heads, nor food, nor money. What do we know about gettin' by in the city?"

"We know a sight more than we did when we first got here, and the bus company is steady work. We'll do okay and, from now on, whatever I do is honest." He reached his hand out again. This time she took it and he pulled her up to stand with his arms around her.

"I hate 'em, Dell. Jesus says it's wrong to hate, but I hate 'em. Alvin Karpis and that idiot Barker woman and her rotten sons, they're bad and they were turnin' you bad with 'em. Mostly I hate Freddie. The way he looks at me and don't say nothin', like he's thinkin' about what all he'd like to do to me."

"That's all through now, honey. I promise. The Greyhound people are making a load of money off this World's Fair. I just happened to walk in at the right time, but the man who hired me said if I wanted work there was plenty of it. I might even get put on at the terminal right over here on Cottage Grove Avenue. Hell, then I could walk to work. Buses can go places where trains don't go. Bus travel is the future and we're in on it." He kissed her and gave her a little pat. "Run on upstairs and wash your face. We're going to the World's Fair tonight. We're going to celebrate."

EIGHTEEN

Gilbert was eager to go up to St. Paul and check out the lead on the woman in the nursing home, but there was one more character in Chicago he wanted to "interview" first, Lefty Egan.

In Alcatraz, Gilbert's father had plied Alvin Karpis with questions about his life of crime and about his life in prison. According to him, back in 1946, Karpis was working in the prison bakery when an oven blew up, throwing flaming oil over his head and arms. He managed to put out the flames but spent several weeks in the prison hospital where he received a morphine drip for the pain. Lefty Egan visited Karpis daily while he was in the hospital, and Gilbert's father was convinced he had taken advantage of Karpis's doped-up condition to grill him about the gold. Egan had been admitted to a nursing home on Chicago's south side immediately after his release from prison, but there was no harm in covering all his bases.

Gilbert piloted his old Taurus down Archer Street to 79th, then cut back east. The Autumn Meadows Residential Care Center was located, uncomfortably, across the street from a cemetery. It was late afternoon, but the summer sun was still bright, and Gilbert was hot and sticky in his tie and jacket. It was a relief to step into the air-conditioned building. He tried to appear official as he strode across the tile floor to the reception desk. Tucked under his arm was a paper-filled clipboard. The receptionist looked up at him and smiled. "May I help you?"

Gilbert glanced around at the beige walls and floor. The sunlight coming through the window gave the room a washed-out appearance. Even the receptionist's blouse and slacks were beige. The only color in the room was a single yellow lily on her desk. He adjusted the drugstore reading glasses on his nose and consulted the clipboard. "I'm here to see a Mr...." He drew his finger down the page. "Ah, here we go. Egan." He handed the receptionist a business card that identified him as an employee of the State of Illinois Department of Healthcare and Family Services. "Mr. Egan has applied for additional financial assistance and we just need to ask him a few questions." Gilbert had to congratulate himself on finding the perfect cover story. The staff at Autumn Meadows would certainly want to help their residents improve their financial health—more for them to poach.

The receptionist escorted Gilbert to an empty seat in the Great Room, a large, high-ceilinged room filled with elderly men and women reading, chatting, and playing cards. The walls were the color of milk chocolate. The carpet was the same washed-out beige as the reception area. In the center of the room stood a stone fireplace and, next to it, a grand piano seemed to be playing itself. Gilbert surveyed the room, eventually fixing his attention on an old woman in a wheelchair. She was sitting near the piano, her eyes closed, swaying back and forth in time to the music. She moved her mouth as though she was singing, but no sound came out. Finally, the receptionist returned with a grizzled-looking old customer in a wheelchair. "I'll just leave you two to chat, shall I? I've got to get back to reception." She kicked the wheelchair's brakes into place and hurried off toward the entrance.

Lefty Egan looked like he hadn't shaved for several days and smelled like he hadn't bathed, either. Gilbert stuck out his hand. "Mr. Egan," he said, "I'm pleased to meet you."

Egan ignored the gesture. "What do you want?" he asked.

"The girl said you were from the government."

"No, sir." Gilbert grinned. "I'm here to ask you about Alvin Karpis." He walked around behind the wheelchair, released the brakes, and started pushing Egan down the hallway, away from the reception area. "You and I are going for a little drive in the country, Mr. Egan. We're going to have a nice little chat about your stay at Alcatraz."

Lefty Egan shouted as loud as his aged lungs would allow. "Help me! Someone help me!" Gilbert punched him in the back of the head.

"Shut up," he said, "or I'll knock you the fuck out." The old convict stopped yelling, but as they approached a side door marked EXIT he threw himself sideways out of the wheelchair. He lay face down on the beige carpet, not moving. As Gilbert reached down to lift him Egan rolled onto his back and slashed Gilbert's hand with a steak knife.

"I may be old but I'm not stupid." He waggled the serrated knife in Gilbert's direction. "I copped this at dinner when I first got here. Come at me again and I'll cut your goddamned throat for you."

Gilbert danced back a few feet, sucking the cut on his hand. "Come on, Mr. Egan, I'm not going to hurt you." He looked around to make sure no one was coming down the hall. "You and me are going to be rich. You just tell me where the Barkers hid all those gold coins, and I'll go fetch them. We'll split fifty-fifty."

Egan squinted up at him from the floor. "Gold coins? So, you think Karpis told me where his old partners hid a bunch of gold coins, eh? Mister, you're crazier than the old coots I have to live with in this geriatric hellhole, and most of them are drooling idiots. Come near me again and I'll carve you a second asshole."

Gilbert looked at the knife and did the only thing he could think of. He picked up the wheelchair and threw it at the old man's head. A wheel rim caught Egan above his left ear. He dropped the knife and collapsed. Gilbert righted the chair, heaved Egan into it, and, as an afterthought, slipped the steak knife into his jacket pocket. Then he kicked open the door and wheeled the convict out into the still-sweltering evening.

Gilbert's "interview" with Lefty Egan had been a bust. Despite further questioning Egan wouldn't admit to knowing anything and Gilbert had wasted an afternoon and a tank of gas driving down to the South Side to see him. He left Egan in a ditch behind the cemetery, staring sightlessly up at the sky.

The drive to St. Paul presented a problem for Gilbert—he was almost out of money. His search of Gertrude Billiter's house had yielded just enough cash to pay for gas to Aurora and his lunch. A burglary was out of the question. Most people didn't keep much money lying around, and it would take too long to fence anything else he might find. It would have to be a robbery.

He had only done a couple of robberies. His dad had been against them; he said they were for boys and idiots, but Gilbert had an idea. It involved some risk, and the payoff wasn't huge, but if done right it was almost a sure thing. He would rob a Starbucks. Liquor stores had cameras and alarm systems, and convenience stores had cash drops behind the counter. Whenever the register in a convenience store had over a hundred dollars in it, the clerk would put the rest in a plastic tube and drop it into a hole in the top of the safe. The clerks never had the combination to the safe, either.

A casual conversation with his neighborhood baristas

---

revealed that Starbucks shops didn't have alarms or safe drops, and only the ones in the city had cameras. Even on a bad day a Starbucks could easily sell a couple thousand dollars' worth of their caffeinated goo. If he went in at the end of the evening he could probably get five hundred out of each register. He knew just which one to rob, too. Robbing a shop in a strip mall would increase the risk because you had to pull out of the parking lot. Depending on the traffic it could add a full minute to his getaway time. But, the Starbucks in downtown Elmhurst was close to the tollway, and it had the added benefit of being on the street. As soon as he got the money, he could hop on the tollway going north to Interstate 94 and ride that all the way to St. Paul.

Gilbert spent the afternoon applying mud to his license plates and shopping for clothes at thrift stores. He wanted a gaudy outfit that would stand out in the clerks' minds more than his facial features. He wasn't worried about other characteristics; there were millions of men his height, weight, and race. As long as they didn't notice his hair or eye color he was okay. He found what he wanted at a place on Halsted Street called the Brown Elephant. He bought a vintage nineteen eighties Members Only jacket with epaulets, an iridescent blue polyester shirt with wide lapels that he wore disco style, outside the jacket, and a lavender ski hat pulled down to cover his wavy brown hair.

It was nine forty-five when he parked his car across from the Starbucks, facing north toward the expressway. Only a handful of customers were still in the shop. There was an elderly couple seated at the window, the man wearing a baseball cap and holding a cane, the woman clutching a straw purse while she sipped her coffee. Three giggling teenage girls were at the counter, just getting their drinks.

Gilbert waited until the girls left, then crossed the street and entered the shop. There were two clerks, college-age boys, behind the counter, and Gilbert smiled when he saw one of them nudge the other and nod his head towards the door. He knew his costume had been noticed. He marched straight up to the counter, taking in the stares of the old couple and the racks of coffee beans, mugs, and compact discs. The two clerks wore green aprons and caps sporting the corporation's ubiquitous logo. One was short, with raven-black hair and a spray-on tan, the other sported a scraggly, blond mustache and goatee. Both wore their hats with the bill in the back. They exchanged smirks as he approached, and the short one moved to the register. "Good evening, sir," he began. "May I help—"

Gilbert smacked him in the mouth with his open palm. The boy staggered back against the steel sink behind him, knocking over a blender and a pitcher of purple liquid. Gilbert had his gun out before the clerk regained his balance.

"You!" He pointed the gun at the other clerk who was standing, open mouthed, behind the espresso machine. "Get over here and join your friend. Keep your mouths shut or die." He tapped the little gun on the counter. "Both of you put your hands on the counter, palms down. Do it now." The two clerks moved to comply, and Gilbert turned to the elderly couple behind him. "Stay in your seats, and keep your hands off your cell phones. If you move, these boys die." He turned back to the first clerk, whose lower lip was starting to swell. "Open this register and put all the paper money in a bag."

The clerk started shaking. His nose was running and his voice cracked when he spoke. "I can't," he said. "The registers won't open without a sale."

Gilbert laughed, then he spoke slowly and methodically. "Okay, genius," he said. "Let's pretend I'm buying a cup of coffee. You ring it up. Then you pretend I'm paying for it with a twenty-dollar bill. The register will open so you can give me my change. You take all the money in the fucking drawer and put it in a fucking bag. That way I don't have to shoot you. Understand?"

The clerk nodded his head and started ringing the sale. Gilbert turned to the boy with the attempted facial hair. "Now you do the same thing with the other register."

In a tiny voice, barely audible, the boy answered, "I'm not logged on." The other clerk spoke up quickly. "I'm the shift manager. I can get on both registers." He handed Gilbert a bag of money and turned to the second register.

"Now you're talking," Gilbert said. "I knew you were a smart boy." He took the second bag from the clerk and tapped his gun on the counter again. "Same as before. Hands on the counter, palms down." He looked at the boy with the mustache. "First though, reach over there and open the valve on that steam wand." He gestured with the gun. The boy turned a knob on the side of the espresso machine, then stepped back to the counter and placed his hands next to his coworker's. The espresso machine hissed, and a cloud of steam billowed out from behind the counter. "That's my favorite part of ordering fancy coffee drinks," Gilbert said. He held up his bags. "That and the free money."

He turned and walked quickly toward the door but, as he approached the elderly couple, he saw the man tighten his grip on his cane and stick his foot out into the aisle. Gilbert stopped in front of him and pressed the barrel of the Beretta against the man's forehead. "This ain't the movies, Pop." The man glared at Gilbert and the woman shook her head and clucked her tongue disapprovingly. Gilbert stepped around them, crossed the street, and drove off toward the tollway.

NINETEEN

McKinney knew he was in trouble when he was summoned with a memo instead of a phone call. It was to be an official meeting. He gathered up his notes on the Drenon and Burdett cases and went downstairs to the director's office. He walked with slow, deliberate steps, pausing in front of the bulletin board in the hallway long enough to read the latest notices. "More birthday cakes and retirement parties," he grumbled. He was like a man walking to the gallows. He closed the office door behind him and slumped into a chair in front of Director Roberts's desk.

The walls in Stanley Roberts's office were covered with awards the director had won when he was a police officer, prior to his appointment as lab director. Most of the awards were for marksmanship, and the shelves and file cabinets held similar trophies. In the middle of the room was an enormous, antique desk, an oak Wooton. Unlike McKinney's messy desk, there wasn't a paper or folder on its polished surface. Stanley Roberts was a year or two older than McKinney, but he was taller and had a more athletic build, the result of daily tennis games. Roberts had the sort of presence McKinney associated with tall, broad-shouldered men who have learned to rely on their looks. McKinney wasn't intimidated by Roberts, but he didn't care much for the director's laissez-faire management style. The lab had a number of problems that McKinney had brought to the director's attention, which he refused to address. This perplexed McKinney. He didn't understand why someone would choose to ignore something that jeopardized the reliability of the lab.

"What's up, Stan?"

"I understand you had a little excitement in court yesterday," the director responded.

According to Nina Anderson, Phillips had been rocking back and forth in the courtroom and mumbling in a fashion typical of autistics. As he became increasingly agitated he had rocked faster and faster, finally rising up and smashing his head down on the wooden table in front of him. He slammed it down over and over, until he passed out. He was in the hospital now, with a broken nose, a fractured skull, and a possible concussion.

"Yeah," McKinney said. "The defendant knocked himself out and had to be hospitalized. The trial was continued. I don't know if they'll keep the same jury or—"

Roberts cut him off. "Why are you working for the public defender?"

McKinney took a deep breath. "I'm not working *for* her. I'm simply testifying to my findings, the same as I would in any other case."

"The State's Attorney's Office doesn't think so. They've called me twice about you, and I also got a call from a Detective Barger. The detective was threatening to charge you with obstruction."

"Charge *me* with obstruction?" McKinney was incredulous. "Apparently I'm the only one who wants to find out what really happened in this case. I've got evidence that indicates the murderer was also involved in another killing. One that took place while this defendant was in jail." He stood up, opened his files on the desk and began shuffling through them, looking for the pictures of the shoeprints. Roberts waved his hands in front of his face to indicate his disinterest.

"It's out of my hands now, McKinney. I talked them out of taking any action against you, but I had to promise I'd have the Department of Internal Investigation look into your conduct. I filed a CADM on you right before I sent you the memo. I just wanted you to know what was happening."

A CADM, or Complaint Against Department Member, was the way to strike fear into the heart of every state police employee, both uniformed and civilian. It meant weeks of answering questions and, for McKinney, trying to explain scientific procedures to investigators who wouldn't understand or care about them. DII officers were used to probing claims of excessive force during an arrest, or investigating employees who said they were working overtime when they were actually hanging out in a neighborhood tavern. They rarely dealt with the intricacies of legal proceedings. These investigations usually ended in a suspension or firing; occasionally criminal charges were filed. McKinney picked up his folders and sat down again.

"Why would you do that without asking for my side of the story? That hardly seems fair."

"I'm not interested in fair, McKinney. I'm interested in why you think you can flaunt laboratory procedure. We're here to work *with* the state's attorneys and the detectives, not against them. What makes you think you have the right to stick your nose where it's not wanted?"

McKinney stared down at the folders on his lap. He was angry now and afraid that, if he looked at Roberts, he'd blow up. He tried to speak calmly, but he could hear his voice quaver. "It's not that I have a right to interfere, I have an obligation. I became a forensic scientist because it gives me the opportunity to search for truth, truth that can help determine who's committed a crime, and sometimes, who hasn't."

"The 'truth' that you seem to have overlooked," Roberts said, "is that the state isn't obliged to disclose evidence they aren't going to use in court. If the defense wanted your report they should have gotten a subpoena."

"There are two things wrong with that argument," McKinney said. "First, if Anderson didn't know my report existed she couldn't subpoena it. Second, the Fifth Amendment of the Constitution says that the government has a duty to reveal favorable evidence to the defense. That was upheld in *Brady v. Maryland* back in 1963, and I think it applies here."

"Oh, brother. Get off your soapbox, McKinney. I know all about Brady, but the judge is supposed to determine what has to be turned over to the defense, not you. Now we're in trouble with the State's Attorney's Office. The last thing I need is to have these guys breathing down my neck."

McKinney shook his head. "When I was in college I had a criminal justice professor who thought crime laboratories should be separate entities, not affiliated with the police in any way. I see what he was getting at now. As long as we think of ourselves as a subsidiary of the police we can never be truly impartial. Science is supposed to be neutral, Stan."

"Well, you can present that theory to the DII officers when they call you in for questioning." Roberts leaned forward. He gripped the edge of his desk with both hands, and his voice became a harsh whisper. "As far as I'm concerned, you're a troublemaker. You've been given a lot of autonomy around here, McKinney. You're always running off to crime scenes or the M.E.'s office to collect your maggots. How often do your bug studies actually make a difference?"

"I've been able to determine approximate time of death on several cases, based on the blowfly larvae."

"Well, I think it's a waste of time. You've been a pain in

my ass for years with all your complaints about coworkers not adhering to policy and your letter to the *Journal of Forensic Sciences* about the dangers of getting false positives because of contamination in the lab."

"And it's those same problems—which you haven't taken the time to address—that prevented the lab from getting certified this year," McKinney retorted. "The lab could squeak by when our certification came from the Association of Crime Laboratory Directors—those guys were all your pals—but with the new national guidelines we have to have ISO certification. It's not so easy when the investigators are from an independent board, is it?"

"Yeah, yeah. You've done your best to make me look bad, McKinney, and I'm sick of you. The choice is yours—get with the program, or I'll get rid of you." Roberts stood, suddenly, and nodded toward the door. "Now you'll have to excuse me. I'm late for an important meeting."

McKinney pushed himself to his feet and trudged back upstairs to his desk in the Trace Evidence Section. A chemist named Gillono caught him at the end of the hallway and tried to recruit him for the lab's softball team. As they talked, McKinney looked out the window and noticed Director Roberts crossing the parking lot, tennis racket and gym bag in hand. *There's his important meeting,* he thought.

When he got back to his desk he saw a yellow sticky-note attached to his telephone. It read "My office" and was signed by his supervisor. *What now?* he thought. He tossed the files onto his desk and tramped across the room.

Vivian Washington looked up from her computer when McKinney entered her office. "Close the door, McKinney. Been having a little heart-to-heart with our illustrious leader, I hear."

"Word travels fast. What's up, Viv?"

She leaned back and gestured to the chair in front of her desk. McKinney sat. "You know that I like having you here in the unit, don't you, McKinney?"

McKinney was surprised. "Sure, I guess so. I mean, thanks."

Vivian lowered her voice. "I'm just going to say this one time, and I'll deny it if you repeat it to anyone. That motherfucker has been gunning for you for months now. You know it, and I know it. Lately he's taken to asking me questions about you, 'How's McKinney's work?' and stuff like that."

"Damn. That guy's like a trapdoor spider."

"A what?"

"A trapdoor spider. He sits in his hole of an office, half blind to the rest of the world, but ready to spring out and sink his fangs in when it suits him."

"Don't give him a reason, McKinney."

"Thanks, Viv."

"On an altogether different topic, did you know that Moses Boadu is married to my cousin, Bernice?"

"Aw, crap. Don't tell me he's pissed off at me, too?"

She smiled and shook her head. The beads at the end of her swinging braids clicked together. "No. Moses likes you. He said you were the kind of guy who could see 'the big picture,' whatever that is. Anyway, he called here, while you were downstairs with the director, and asked me to tell you about a murder. A friend of his, an Aurora cop named Davis, told him they recently had an old lady killed out there."

"Will *we* get the evidence, or will it go to the Joliet lab?"

"I haven't seen any of the evidence come into the lab yet but, if I do, I'll make sure it's assigned to you." She handed McKinney a slip of paper. "Here's the cop's phone number, in case you want to talk to him. Moses says he's a good guy."

"That's what he said about Barger and that guy's an ass. Sorry. I'm just in a bad mood. Thank Detective Boadu for me if you see him."

McKinney walked back to his desk and sat, staring at the phone number on the paper. Roberts had given him a clear choice, conform or be fired. He ought to throw the paper away and forget about it. A hit-and-run case had come in that morning. He ought to start working on that. He ought to just forget about Phillips and dead senior citizens and tear up the phone number. Jameson and Barger didn't care if they had the real killer as long as they got a conviction. Anderson hadn't told him that Phillips was taking haloperidol. Why should he stick his neck out? He crumpled the slip of paper in his fist and tossed it into the wastebasket.

TWENTY

Delroy was just taking a piece of leftover fried chicken out of the icebox when the door to the little apartment flew open. A man he had never seen before stumbled in, followed by Freddie Barker and his brother Doc.

"Hey, Dell," said Freddie. "Glad you're home."

The unknown man stood in the middle of the room holding his hat and rubbing his bald head. He was pudgy and pasty-faced and wore a three-piece, brown suit that looked like it had been slept in. Delroy caught a whiff of something that smelled like vomit. Freddie pushed him into a straight-backed chair.

"Sit, you."

Delroy put the chicken leg down on the oilcloth-covered table and wiped his fingers on his undershirt. *Damn*, he thought. *Damn, damn.*

"H'lo Freddie, Doc. What gives?" Delroy noticed a bandage across Doc Barker's nose. It was stained brown. "You boys okay?"

Doc Barker walked past the kitchenette into the living area and threw himself onto the sofa. He took a small flask out of his coat pocket and drank deep. The man in the chair watched him for a second, then stared down at the hat in his hands. Freddie straddled a chair at the kitchen table and picked up Delroy's chicken leg.

"I'm about half starved, Dell. Your missus home?"

"She took a job waiting tables down to Merkle's diner. I just got home from work, myself. Where've you all been? You left town and the first I knew about it was when I heard Mrs.

Finch complain to Lucille she'd lose a month's rent 'cause no one would be looking for a place so close to Christmas." He pointed to the man in the chair. "Who's this?"

Doc lay back on the camelback sofa and moaned. Freddie tossed the picked-clean chicken bone on the table and looked at the man in the chair. "This, Dell, is the late Joseph P. Moran. He claims he's a doctor."

Doc lifted his head from the embroidered pillow he'd found and shouted at the man in the chair, "Butcher!" Moran hunched over and concentrated on his hat.

"We paid him to fix our faces and wipe out our fingerprints, but he botched the job. I didn't let him touch my face after I saw what he done to Doc and Alvin. Oh, brother, wait'll you see Alvin."

"He's here?"

"He's parking the car. He'll be up in a minute. We need a place to hole up for a couple of days."

"Oh, I don't know, Freddie. I'd like to let you stay but, well, you know Lucille hates Alvin. He scares her something awful."

"Him and Doc'll stay at my girl Paula's place with Ma, but I need you to help me keep an eye on this fish 'til I figure out what to do with him."

"What do you mean?"

"He drinks. He drinks and then he runs his mouth."

Moran looked up at Freddie.

"It was only a couple of whores, Freddie, and they won't talk. Anyway I'm on the straight and narrow now. I won't say another word to anyone."

Freddie took one step toward Moran and punched him in the ear. Moran caught himself before he fell out of the chair. Doc looked up, snorted, and lay back, closing his eyes.

"Damn right you won't. If Edith hadn't told me what her girls was talking about you'd have kept flapping your gums until the bulls knew everything but my shoe size. And quit fooling with your damn hat," Freddie said. He held his hand up to examine his knuckles. The middle one was starting to swell. "You make me nervous."

Delroy hadn't seen the Barkers in over six months. He'd worked lookout on two more jobs for them after the St. Paul post office heist, before he went to work for Greyhound. No one had been shot on those jobs, but he wasn't sorry when they moved out. He picked a pot off the stove and started to fill it at the sink.

"I'll make us coffee. Lucille can cook some eggs or something when she gets home."

"You surely are a lucky bastard, Dell. That little redhead's a fine woman."

"Yeah," Delroy said, "lucky." He opened a cupboard to get out the cups. The paint on the cupboard door was cracked and peeling, and he started to pick at it while he thought. He'd got them in a real mess. Lucille hated the Barkers. What if she shot her mouth off? These boys were dangerous. There was no telling what they'd do. What if Freddie wanted help killing this Moran? What if he refused? He'd thought they were out of it, and now here was Freddie again with his scary eyes.

The hissing and spitting of the water on the stove startled him. There was a pile of paint chips on the sink. Delroy tugged his shirtsleeve down over his hand and used it as a potholder while he poured the water.

"We got sugar but no milk."

Freddie chuckled. "That's okay, Dell. I'll take mine hot and sweet, just like my women."

The front door swung open and Freddie's hand darted to

his hip, then relaxed. A man with bandages on his face and hands stood in the doorway, gripping an angry Lucille by the arm. It was Alvin Karpis.

"Looky who I met downstairs," he said.

TWENTY-ONE

Gilbert parked the maroon Taurus in the afternoon shade on an empty, tree-lined street, two blocks north of The Little Sisters nursing home, in rural River Bend, Minnesota. The only building on the block was a burned-out, deserted gas station. On the other side of the street was an open field.

Back in Aurora, Gertrude Billiter hadn't been able to shed any light on the whereabouts of the Barker/Karpis gang's hidden gold, though Gilbert felt she had sincerely tried. Even before he started beating her daughter, she told him about several of Harry Campbell's associates in the 1930s. She talked about Volney Davis and his crazy girlfriend, Edna "The Kissing Bandit" Murray. She'd met Jean Delaney, the sister of Karpis's girlfriend Delores Delaney, and "Baby Face" Nelson and his wife Helen. Her list of famous gangster acquaintances was long and illustrious, but the only one she thought might still be alive was Viola Nordquist. Viola had been a hatcheck girl at the Hollyhocks Club in St. Paul and the girlfriend of Jack Peifer, the club's owner and a local fixer. He'd made St. Paul a hospitable town for gangsters by greasing the palms of St. Paul's cops and politicians. Peifer also helped the Barkers engineer the kidnapping of the heir to the Hamm's Beer fortune, a business enterprise that earned him a thirty-year sentence. But, instead of doing his time, he committed suicide.

Peifer's death had drained all the life out of Viola. She never married. She continued working at the Hollyhocks for a few years, then drifted from one menial job to the next until she was no longer able to fend for herself. Gertrude had received a letter from her just last year. Fortunately for Gilbert, she'd saved both the letter and the envelope.

Gilbert didn't enjoy killing Gertrude as much as he'd enjoyed his other murders. Reading her diary and meeting her daughter made him feel like he'd gotten to know her but, by this time, he considered killing the people he "interviewed" a business necessity. He couldn't risk being identified. He did Gertrude the courtesy of shooting her first so she wouldn't have to see him shoot her daughter.

He'd phoned the nursing home from Chicago and the receptionist confirmed that Viola Nordquist was, indeed, still living there. Gilbert drove up that same night, but he hadn't figured out how to approach the task at hand. He considered a variety of scenarios on the way, but none were without risk and several were just stupid. Masquerading as a doctor or family member was the sort of thing you'd see on a TV show, but he knew the chances of that working were slim to none. He didn't have those kinds of acting skills and, even if he did, there were dozens of ways it could go wrong. He was reluctant to use his "government employee" routine again.

He glanced at the bandage on the back of his hand. That had just barely worked on Lefty Egan. Breaking in after hours was a possibility, but if the old lady screamed there'd be nurses or staff to contend with. Taking her out of there seemed the most likely idea, but Gilbert didn't know what machines she might be hooked up to. If she was on a ventilator, or had an IV in her arm, he'd have to unplug her to move her. What if she needed the stuff to live? He just didn't have enough information to figure it out, and he didn't want to go in blind, it was too risky. He'd been stymied by that problem with Lefty Egan, and hesitating had almost cost him his life. He'd run into a number of problems lately, and he couldn't chalk them all up to bad luck. Some of it had undoubtedly been due to poor planning. Well, no more. Since he needed information, he would have to buy it.

The evening before he'd followed one of the staff—a man who looked like a janitor—home to his apartment a few blocks down the street. He was surprised at how readily the man, Terrell, had accepted his offer of fifty bucks in return for the information he wanted.

Now he lowered all the car's windows to let in the breeze and took a box of fig cookies and a root beer out of a plastic bag on the passenger seat. He hadn't gotten as much from the Starbucks robbery as he'd hoped, but he'd have to kill the janitor to eliminate the risk of exposure and he could recover the money then. He glanced at his watch. It was ten minutes until the end of Terrell's shift, so Gilbert sat back to wait. *This treasure hunt*, he thought, *is turning into a wild goose chase.* He doubted that Viola Nordquist would know any more about the money than the other seniors, and he was starting to think that the whole deal was a waste of time.

He'd done things that put him in greater danger than his usual burgling; killing little old ladies was sure to be looked at unfavorably by a jury, even if they had been gun molls. Besides, he wasn't sure how he felt about it. It was important to cover his tracks, but killing someone was different from swiping a lockbox of jewelry. He thought most killers had probably been cruel when they were children. He'd known kids who pulled the legs off insects to see them squirm, or thrown rocks at stray cats. Those kids had disgusted him, yet here he was, killing people and enjoying it. He was looking forward to killing Terrell right now, and the excitement of his anticipation was mixed with self-loathing. If he didn't get worthwhile information out of Viola Nordquist, he decided, he would give up the hunt. When decisions were influenced by anything other than business considerations it was time to reevaluate. He took a swig of root beer and spat it out the window. It had gone warm in the afternoon heat.

He saw the janitor sauntering up the street toward him, trailing a long shadow until he came under the shade of the trees. Gilbert felt the weight of the gun in his pocket and was glad to have it; Terrell was a shorthaired, square-jawed man who looked like he spent his evenings at the gym. When he slid into the passenger seat the Taurus dipped a couple of inches.

"Got what you want, man. Let's have some cash."

Gilbert took out his wallet and handed him three tens and a twenty. "So?"

Terrell slipped the bills into his shirt pocket. "Miz Nordquist is in room 1057, first floor, at the back. Here's a little map I drew, like you asked. She has one of those oxygen tubes under her nose, but that's it. Her teeth don't fit her, so she don't eat much solid food, but she drinks a couple cans of supplement every day."

"No IVs or anything like that?" Gilbert asked.

"Nope. I don't know what you intend to do, but I don't guess anyone'd be sorry if somethin' was to happen to her. That's one cranky bitch."

Gilbert slid his wallet into his back pocket, then quickly shoved his hand into his front pocket and pulled out the Beretta. He pushed the gun against Terrell's chest and pulled the trigger. The little .25 caliber bullet didn't find the heart. The janitor bellowed with pain and surprise, and brought his fist down on Gilbert's arm, before he could fire again. Then, he held Gilbert's gun hand against the seat and hit him in the face, over and over again. Suddenly, Gilbert was confused. He couldn't see past the pain and the pummeling fist. He felt the cartilage in the bridge of his nose give way as he fumbled for the door handle with his free hand. The door swung open behind him, and he fell backward, out of the car, his weight pulling Terrell across the driver's seat. Gilbert's vision cleared when he hit the ground, and he saw the janitor's face in front of him. It was a face contorted with anger, fear, and pain, the eyes wide and white, lips pulled away from snarling teeth, spit flying as he screamed. Gilbert pulled his gun hand free, aimed at the demon, and fired.

TWENTY-TWO

McKinney was cutting up a butternut squash at the kitchen counter when he heard his cell phone ring in the other room. The enthusiasm with which he attacked the vegetable was a product of his anger. He was mad at Roberts for siccing the DII on him and at Anderson for not telling him about the haloperidol. Mostly he was angry with himself for getting drawn into a case beyond his field of expertise.

The temptation to solve crimes was a constant with forensic scientists, and he understood, even if he disapproved of, his peers' attempts to emulate Sherlock Holmes. He regularly rejected requests from attorneys to give inappropriate weight to his testimony. Occasionally one would try to blindside him on the witness stand. Most often it was the prosecution who wanted him to say that the presence of gunshot residue on a suspect's hands was proof the person had fired a weapon. When this happened McKinney would patiently explain to the jury that the presence of gunshot residue indicated one of three things—the suspect had fired a weapon, had been in the vicinity when a weapon was fired, or had contact with a weapon after it was fired. Generally this explanation was delivered while the state's attorney glared at him.

He stabbed the knife, ice pick-style, into the squash and went to answer his phone. It was Nina Anderson.

"I'm not happy with you," McKinney said.

"What? Why not?"

"You didn't tell me that your client is medicated. That he takes haloperidol."

"I didn't think it was important. I know the distinction may seem small to a jury but Phillips is autistic, not schizophrenic. He doesn't need the medication to stop delusions. He doesn't have delusions."

"But taking it affects his behavior. I just think you should have told me."

There was silence on the phone, then, "You're right. I'm sorry. Had you known, would you have decided not to help?"

McKinney thought for a moment. "I don't know. I'm getting some heavy pushback for my involvement in the case, and I'm a little worried about my job. I'm not exactly the most popular guy at the lab right now."

"I'm sorry to hear that. If there's anything I can do…"

"Thanks," McKinney said. "So, what's up?"

"I have a friend in the medical examiner's office who told me about a decomp that came in the other day with similar characteristics to Mr. Drenon and the other case you told me about."

"Decomp, eh. How bad?"

"She doesn't think it was outdoors more than a week. It's a man. Some homeless guys found him. No ID yet but my friend thinks they can still get fingerprints from his hands."

"Why do you think it's related to my murders?"

"I have a copy of the M.E.'s report on this guy. I'd like to show it to you, get your take on it. Can you meet me after work?"

"I probably shouldn't."

"I'll buy you a drink…"

They decided to meet at Katerina's, one of Nina Anderson's favorite haunts in the Old Irving Park neighborhood. She was already seated when McKinney arrived, and as he sat he noticed she was wearing the blue cousin to the green silk blouse she had on the day she came to the crime lab. He thought there was an extra button undone this time. An almost-empty glass sat on the table in front of her.

"What are you drinking?" he asked.

"Campari and soda. Want one?"

"No thanks." He flagged down the waitress and ordered a gin and tonic for himself and another Campari for her. As the waitress went to fill the order, he looked around the room. It was long and narrow with dark wood and white tablecloths. The bar ran the length of one wall, and a small stage and a baby grand piano were at the far end of the room. A woman in a black evening gown was doing her best to sound like Billie Holiday as she warbled "Good Morning Heartache." McKinney turned his attention back to the public defender. She was aligning the silverware. "This is the first time I've been here, Counselor. It's nice."

"Please," she said, "call me Nina. Yeah, it has a sort of relaxed elegance, plus I live nearby so I don't have to drive. I thought you might get a kick out of the singer. Her name is Cricket and you're an entomologist, so..." McKinney smiled at her. "Well, I guess that is kind of lame. Anyway, thanks for meeting me." She pulled her briefcase from under the table and rummaged around inside until she found the file she wanted. "Here—they identified him this afternoon, ran his fingerprints through AFIS. He was an old gangster named Lefty Egan. He did some time at Alcatraz. He was shot in the head, twice. From the pictures it looks like he was tortured, too."

McKinney opened the file. Staring up at him from the first photograph was a Caucasian male, bald, with a gray mustache. His face didn't show much decomposition but it was puffy. McKinney estimated that the man had been in his seventies or eighties. On the man's right cheek was a faint pattern, a shoeprint. McKinney studied it, looking for the impression of a damaged lug. He didn't find one and couldn't remember enough other details to tell if the pattern looked the same as the shoeprints from the other cases. Still...

"Can I hang on to this for a couple of days?" he asked.

Nina smiled. "I was hoping you would."

McKinney closed the file and slid it off to one side of the table. The waitress brought their drinks and Nina drained the glass in her hand and swapped it for the fresh one. "What made you decide to go into forensic science?" she asked.

This was a question McKinney had asked himself often, and he didn't pause to think before answering. "When I was an undergrad I had to pick a couple of elective courses to fill out my schedule. One of them was an intro to criminalistics class. We took a tour of a crime lab and went to the M.E.'s office to watch an autopsy. That was fun—three students passed out when they removed the brain. What hooked me, though, was my professor's definition of forensic science. 'Law is man's attempt to civilize society. Science is man's attempt to reveal truth. Forensic science then, is the intersection of civilization and truth.' I like the idea of having a job that lets me look for truth." He sipped his drink. "How about you?"

"You mean, why criminal law? I guess I was interested in justice. I used to think I'd be bored in any other branch of the profession—contract law, patents, whatever. These days boredom looks mighty appealing. Did you know I used to work for the State's Attorney's Office?"

"No. When was that?"

"A few years ago. That's one of the reasons Brian Jameson and I don't get along. He thinks I defected to the other team."

"You don't see it that way?"

"No, I don't. After years of prosecuting cases I began to

realize that most of the people I was sending to prison weren't being given a proper defense. Most of them were probably guilty, but even so, the state's resources were overwhelming compared to what the defendants were getting from the overworked Public Defender's Office. There was a big, ol' thumb on the scale of justice. I just wanted to even things up a little." She picked up her glass and looked at McKinney through the red liquid. "Now, I don't know. I'm not sure real justice is possible. Some of the people I defend wind up getting a raw deal, while others should just be tossed in a deep, dark pit." She took a drink. "Not Phillips, though. That kid never killed anyone."

McKinney excused himself to use the washroom. He had to walk past the little stage where Cricket was crooning "Stormy Weather." *Too true*, he thought. It had dawned on him that this was more like a date than a business meeting, and, inexplicably, his thoughts turned to Carla, rather than Catherine. *That's just great*, he thought. *Now I've got two reasons to feel guilty.* On the way back to the table Cricket winked at him, ratcheting his discomfort up another notch. When he returned there were fresh drinks on the table, and Nina was sitting with her hands clenched in her lap, staring down at the table. She had sorted all the sweetener packets by color and lined them up next to the silverware.

"Nervous?" McKinney asked.

She didn't turn her head but kept looking at the table. "I couldn't stop myself. Usually drinking relaxes me, gives me something to do with my hands. I'm really embarrassed."

"Don't be, I don't mind."

"It was worse when I was a child. That was before teachers understood obsessive-compulsive disorders. They just thought I was strange. My classmates, of course, thought so, too. I don't know which was worse, getting sent home from school for being a 'disruptive influence' or staying in class. The other kids were always imitating my behaviors."

McKinney tried to see her face, but wings of her long blonde hair hid it from him. "What kind of behaviors?"

"Mostly touching—objects, not people. I had to touch various objects and always in the same sequence. If I didn't get to touch them I'd become agitated. First, the number plate on my locker, three times, then the doorknob on the janitor's closet, a hinge on the door to my classroom, the seat of my chair, three times, my books, in order by size, smallest first, three times each. While the teacher was talking I would keep my pink eraser on my desk. I touched that almost constantly. I was usually asked to leave the room if the touching got too loud or if the kids started laughing. Occasionally I was compelled to leave my seat and touch the pencil sharpener or bookcase or, if I couldn't remember whether I'd touched my locker the three necessary times, I'd have to go out into the hall and start over." She let out a loud sigh and worked her shoulders back and forth, trying to relax them. "It's so much better now, but every once in a while... Now I mostly just straighten things, organize them."

McKinney tried to lighten the mood. "You must have the cleanest apartment in the world."

"You'd think so, wouldn't you? It's a pigsty. There are stacks of papers and books everywhere. All their edges are neatly lined up, but there isn't one unused surface in the whole place." She turned to McKinney and gave him an apologetic smile. "Sorry. Can we talk about something non-humiliating?"

They chatted until almost eleven. Then McKinney walked her the two blocks to her apartment. On the way back to his car he saw Cricket standing in front of the nightclub, smoking a cigarette.

"That can't be good for your voice," McKinney said.

"You and my mother," she snapped, "can both go to hell."

McKinney finally admitted that sleep wasn't in his immediate future. He couldn't get his mind to stop replaying the events of the last couple of days. Finally, he turned over in bed once too often and his feet tangled in the covers. He kicked them off, pulled on a pair of pants, and huffed out to the kitchen for a beer. Then he went to the hall closet. He dug past the winter coats, and the vacuum, and the ironing board that no one used anymore, and brought out a beat-up cardboard box. He carried it and his beer into the dimly lit living room, put on some B.B. King and settled himself on the couch. Hendrix followed him in from the bedroom, lay at his feet on the Persian rug, and immediately started snoring.

The box had originally contained the little television he and Catherine bought when they were first married. Now it held the detritus of his past—photographs, love letters, birthday cards, even a scrap of fabric from Catherine's wedding dress. It had been a kind of hippie wedding, out in a forest preserve, with both of them dressed in white linen. Her dress had a flower embroidered over the heart. The scrap of material with the embroidery was all that remained, the rest of the dress having been turned into a little outfit for baby Angelina. He pressed it against his cheek and breathed in the scent of melancholy.

At the wedding they'd danced a tarantella. Catherine's mother brought the music, and she gathered everyone in a circle and demonstrated the dance while she explained its folk origins. In southern Italy, she said, people used to believe that if a tarantula bit you, you could dance away the effects of the

---

venom. The tarantula dance was frenzied and wild and long. You had to keep dancing to forestall death. McKinney, the drunken scientist, tried to tell them that a tarantula bite would be unlikely to kill an adult and that dancing wouldn't help the victim, anyway. Catherine told him to shut up and dance; then she took his hand and pulled him into the circle.

McKinney took a long swallow of beer and set the fabric aside. He dug past the photos to the bundles of letters at the bottom. The first packet he pulled out were letters Catherine had written to him while he was in graduate school. He'd read them so often since her death that he didn't really need to open them. He picked the top one from the stack. *Postmarked in January*, he thought. *This one was written from her parents' house in Arizona. She teases me about the weather, it's warm there, and in Chicago we've just been socked in by a blizzard.* He flipped through the stack until he found the letter he was looking for. He slid it from its envelope and unfolded it.

Hey Babe,

I've thunk and thunk and, as hard as I try, I just can't come up with a good reason not to marry you. I'm sorry I made you wait, but I had to be certain you're the only man I'll ever love... so I called several thousand men (sorry about the phone bill, Mom and Dad) and gave them a short quiz. It consisted of just one question, "Are you the guy for me?" I received a variety of answers, mostly along the lines of, "Who is this?" but after all the responses were tallied I think I was able to extrapolate (look, a big word!) a conclusion. Part of your forensic science curriculum involves statistics, doesn't it? Well, my statistics tell me that you're the

only guy I ever want to share my bed with so,
yes, yes, yes!
I love you,
Catherine
P.S. We need to share that bed soon!

He folded the letter and set it next to the box on the coffee table. Before her death the letter had made him grin. Now, when he read it, his chest was filled with sharp things, making it hard to breathe. He thought back to the months after she died. He had been enveloped in numbness, like he was peering out at the world through layers of spun glass or cotton. He found it difficult to do anything. Even lifting his arms required a massive effort. Eventually, lethargy gave way to anger. It wasn't much of an improvement. He hadn't cried once in the two years since his wife's death, and he was ashamed. He felt like a fraud. Maybe this pain in his chest signaled some kind of progress. He leaned back on the couch and looked up, not at the ceiling but beyond it. "I'm so sorry, Catherine," he said. Experimentally, he tried to force a sob. It didn't catch.

He rubber-banded the letters and put them back in the box. A faded yellow envelope caught his eye as he was closing the box's cardboard flaps. He pulled it out and sniffed. It had the same musty smell he remembered from childhood explorations of his grandmother's attic. In the envelope was a birthday card with a picture of a clown beating a drum with a big "3" on it. McKinney opened the card. It read, "Happy birthday, big boy, from Grandma and Grandpa!" There was a slip of folded paper in the card. He started to unfold it when he noticed Angelina standing in the hallway, rubbing her eyes. McKinney turned the volume down on B.B.'s version of "Someday Baby."

"Did I wake you?" he asked.

"What are you doing up, Dad?"

"Just looking through some stuff. Hey, I found a birthday card your great-grandparents sent me when I was only three years old." He held out the card and Angelina stumbled over and plopped down next to him on the couch.

"Was it written on parchment?" she asked. "They didn't have paper back then, did they?"

"What a clever girl you are." He handed her the card and unfolded the slip of paper. "Hey, they sent me a poem, too."

> *Little Sean, you're three today*
> *You're daddy's pride and joy*
> *Your mommy loves you lots and lots*
> *You're her special little boy*
> *But there's two more folks who think*
> *That you're the cat's meow.*
> *Your Grandma Lucy and your old Grand-Pap*
> *We love you too, and how!*

"Pee-eeeuw." Angelina held her nose. "That stinks."

"Well, then, you better hope you didn't inherit your poetry-writing skills from my side of the family."

"Oh, my God! Don't even joke about that. Did you really call him Grand-pap?"

"I don't know. I don't remember my grandfather very well. He died when I was about five."

"Don't forget, we're going to see Great-grandma in two weeks."

"I haven't forgotten."

"Why are you looking at this stuff now? It's two in the morning."

"I couldn't sleep. I kept thinking about the Phillips case. I think it's likely that the guy's innocent but the investigator in charge of the case and the prosecution both have him pegged as the killer. I'm supposed to remain impartial, but I don't think he's getting a fair shake."

Angelina turned sideways on the couch and stuck her bare feet under her father's leg. McKinney smiled. It was the way she used to sit as a little girl, the two of them reading together on the couch.

"This is the guy who's autistic, right?" she asked.

"Yep, and the only thing that can help him is to catch the real killer. I think he's still out there somewhere, but I haven't found anything that would give us a clue to his identity. The best evidence I've found, so far, is a blood smear on a glass chip. I gave it to Amy in the DNA unit, and she got a good profile from it. We ran the results through the CODIS database but didn't get any hits."

"So, what are you going to do?"

"I don't know. His lawyer asked me for help, but really, I've done my job. If I start investigating on my own I'll probably end up in hot water. I could even get fired."

"Well, like Mom always used to say, only the deluded and the fearful sacrifice truth for comfort. You'll think of something." She poked him in the ribs with her toe. "You always do. Hey, how are things going with Mrs. Reyes?"

McKinney groaned. "I said something stupid and she took it the wrong way."

Angelina sat up straight and grinned at her father. "So... you like her, don't you?"

"Yeah, I like her. We were getting along okay, too, until I started talking about your mother. I got tongue-tied."

"Dad, women don't want to hear about other women. You should apologize and ask her out on another date."

"I guess." He studied Angelina's face, looking for any indication of resentment. "Are you okay with me dating someone...you know...besides your mother? I think most kids your age would feel hurt or jealous. It doesn't bother you?"

"It bothers me that you're so sad all the time. I miss Mom a lot, but I want you to be happy. You're more fun to be around when you're happy."

McKinney took the yellow envelope from his daughter, replaced the poem and tossed it into the box. "In case I haven't mentioned it lately…you are a wonderful human being. Hey, on a different note, how's school? Did you finish that book you were reading?"

"Yeah. I finished the report, too. I hand it in tomorrow. And my chem lab partner, Janice, and I are doing a science project together. You'd be proud of us."

"What is it?"

"We're using electrolysis to generate hydrogen. You know, to show how easy it is to make an alternative fuel for a car."

"Cool, very cool. And how's that boy you like, Richard?"

"We broke up. I told you that."

"You did? I guess I forgot. Anyone else on the horizon?"

"I don't know." Angelina got up and started for the hallway. "I should get to bed, school tomorrow, you know."

"Hey, wait. That's not fair. How come you get to know who I'm dating, but you won't tell me what's going on with you?"

"I'm sorry. I'm just not comfortable discussing my love life with my father."

"What do you mean 'love life'? You can't have a love life. You're too young to have a love life."

"Good night, Dad."

He called after her. "You're not allowed to have a love life!"

McKinney went into his bedroom and retrieved his wedding ring from the nightstand next to his bed. He wrapped it in the piece of embroidered fabric from his wife's wedding dress, placed it in the box of photos and returned the box to the closet.

TWENTY-THREE

The newspapers seemed to think that Ma Barker was the brains behind the Barker/Karpis gang, but Delroy knew that was just something they cooked up to sell papers. She was a dumb Okie who believed her boys weren't as bad as the press made them out to be. Doc and Freddie accounted for whatever brains there were and Karpis was sort of the drill sergeant. He recruited and supervised the other men they used on their various jobs.

It was Freddie who took Moran for a little ride in the country one sunny Sunday afternoon. He came back that evening, alone. Delroy was relieved Freddie hadn't asked him to go along, but it made him ill to think of the terror Moran must have felt, riding along with Freddie chattering away and knowing the whole time he was going to die. When he got back, Freddie opened a bottle of beer he'd bought on the way and pulled a chair up to the kitchen table where Delroy and Lucille were eating dinner.

"Lord almighty," he said. "It's a hot day to be out there digging a hole in the ground."

"Shut up, Freddie," Lucille said.

Freddie took off his shirt and draped it over the back of his chair. He wore a sleeveless undershirt and, on top of that, a black leather shoulder rig holding a heavy-looking gun. He put the beer bottle to his lips, tipped it straight up and drank. When he put the bottle down he looked at Lucille and grinned. "He started crying in the car on the way there. I never seen a grown-up man cry before, and I sure hope I never have to see it again."

"I told you to shut up," Lucille said. She looked at Delroy. "This is cold-blooded murder, pure and simple. I won't have us messed up in it, and I won't have a murderer in my home. I want him out of here right now."

"Are you gonna let Little Red talk to us like that, Dell?" Freddie asked.

Delroy looked at Freddie and back at Lucille and knew that there was no answer he could give that wouldn't start a ruckus. He hated Freddie now. Hated him for being what Delroy had known he was all along. He hated Freddie for the way he talked to Lucille and for the way he would leer at her right in front of him, as if it didn't matter that he was her husband and right there in the same room. He couldn't even protect her in his own home. *Hell*, he thought, *even if I get Freddie's gun away from him, it won't solve anything. I can't shoot anyone, not even Freddie, and if I toss him out he'll just come back with another gun and his brother...or Karpis.* All he could do was hope Lucille would hush up and that neither of them got too hot under the collar.

"Freddie," he said, "it's no matter that you and me are friends. Lucille is my wife and I've got to respect her wishes."

"Well, I'm sorry to hear you say that, Dell. Me and Ma and the boys are going down to our place in Florida tomorrow, and I was gonna invite you and Little Red to go with us. You read about that guy Edward Bremer in the papers, didn't you? You know, the one who got himself kidnapped and had to cough up two hundred grand? That was our job, boy. We're sitting pretty, and I got a place that the law don't know about. You all are welcome to come on down and live it up some." He reached into the shoulder holster, pulled out his .45 automatic and laid it on the table in front of him. "I think the climate would be good for your health."

Delroy watched the gun as he spoke. "That's a generous offer, Freddie. I think me and Lucille should sleep on it. Either way, we surely aren't in the habit of turning our friends out in the middle of the night. We'll probably all feel better in the morning, anyway." He turned to Lucille. "Honey, I bet Freddie's hungry after his…um…his long drive. Why don't you fix him a plate?"

Lucille glared at them both and went to the stove. She spooned a serving of stew onto a clean plate and put it in front of Freddie, next to his gun. "I'll get you a fork," she said.

"Thank you, ma'am. It smells tasty. Maybe you and me should go to Florida and leave ol' Dell here. I ain't such a bad sort, once you get to know me." As she turned he patted her on the behind. Delroy clenched his fists beneath the table while he struggled to keep his face impassive.

Lucille walked over to the kitchenette and pulled open a drawer next to the sink. When she turned back she was holding a little .32 caliber revolver. Freddie made a grab for his automatic just as Lucille started firing. Delroy beat him to it and snatched the gun off the table. He kicked himself over backwards in his chair before Freddie could jump him. The little revolver sounded six sharp cracks as Lucille emptied it, managing to take off a piece of Freddie's right ear.

"She shot me, Dell. The little whore shot me!" Freddie was on his feet, hopping up and down and holding his ear. Blood dripped from between his fingers onto the floorboards.

Delroy untangled himself from the chair and stood up, covering Freddie with the automatic. His voice quavered when he spoke, and he struggled to sound calm and in control. "I'm sorry, Freddie. I guess we're not going with you to Florida after all. Considering the rough feelings here tonight, you'd best go on. Lucille, honey, get Freddie some alcohol and bandages for his ear."

Lucille was shaking and the acrid smell of the discharged gun started her coughing. She went into the bathroom and came out with a handful of towels. She tossed them at Freddie from the far side of the kitchen table. "Take 'em and get."

Freddie pressed the towels to his ear. Red soaked through the fabric.

"Hold on a minute," Delroy said. He knew from the maniacal look on Freddie's face that this wasn't over. He had to find some way to calm him down. "Freddie, sit down a second. Lucille, honey, bring me your little revolver and that box of cartridges from the kitchen drawer." Delroy loaded the .32 and unloaded Freddie's automatic. He slid the automatic across the table.

"You'll probably need this, Freddie. I'm sorry about your ear, but it could have been worse. She could have made you drink her coffee."

Freddie slipped his gun back into its holster with his free hand, then picked up his shirt. He skewered Delroy with a cold grin. "You're a funny boy when you're holding the only loaded gun, ain'tcha? Well, so long you two. I'll be seein' ya."

As soon as he was out the door Delroy slipped the .32 into his pocket and ushered Lucille to the fire escape. "We're going out the back way. There's no telling what he's got in his car—Tommy guns, grenades, howitzers. We'll spend the night down by the lake."

As they trotted down the alley Delroy became aware of Lucille's hand in his. He loosened his grip, experimentally, and she tightened hers. When he judged they were far enough away from the apartment he stopped and pulled her into the shadow of a building. He could feel the cold grit of the bricks on his back. They were across from the Thirty-First Street entrance to the World's Fair. Past the gates they could see the Mayan temple exhibit, its silhouette outlined by the glow from the fair behind it.

"You were pretty good back there, honey," he said. "You've got a lot of gumption."

"Gumption, hell! I was scared to death." She reached up and touched Delroy's cheek. Her hand was still shaking. "We won't be shed of them until they're dead or in jail," she said. "Tomorrow we contact the law."

"I can't squeal on them, Lucille."

"Well, I can and I will. I'll do whatever it takes to protect my family."

"Family?" he asked. She looked up at him. The lights from the World's Fair shone on her face and her eyes were the greenest he'd ever seen them. She smiled and pulled his face down to hers. Delroy could feel the electricity in her kiss. He made it last a long time.

TWENTY-FOUR

Gilbert regretted his decision to kill the janitor for several reasons, not the least of which was the man's weight. His intention was to stash the body in the middle of the field across from the abandoned gas station. It was convenient, there was no traffic, and the grass and weeds were at least waist high. He'd have to carry him, though. Dragging him out there would flatten the grass, making a trail straight to the body.

Fortunately, the man had fallen out of the car when Gilbert shot him so there was very little blood on the seats. He didn't want to get blood on his clothes either, so he pulled the bag that had held his root beer and cookies over the janitor's head and placed the passenger-side floormat against his chest. He jockeyed the corpse into a sitting position, slipped his head under its armpit and, pushing off the side of the car for leverage, managed to get the body up and over his shoulder. Then, he straightened his legs and staggered out into the field. Tall prairie grasses roiled like waves on an ocean, engulfing his legs. The sun was hot, and he hoped the dampness on his back was only perspiration. "Fuckin' heavy motherfucker," he grunted. He counted off fifty steps and let the body slide off his shoulder, to be swallowed by the rippling grass.

Exhausted, he headed back to his motel to clean up and, as he drove, he became aware of the other reason he shouldn't have killed him. The back and side doors at The Little Sisters nursing home would be locked. The janitor could have let him in, unobserved. Now he would have to break in.

His face began to ache, and he twisted the rearview mirror

to assess the damage. His nose was flattened to his cheek and dripping blood. He pulled into a strip mall and parked at the far end, away from the other cars. He couldn't tell if it was broken or not, but a doctor was out of the question. He dug around in the glove compartment until he found a pencil, which he wedged between his nose and cheek. He raised the car windows to muffle the noise, gripped the pencil with both hands, and braced his thumbs against his cheekbones. Taking a deep breath, he jerked the pencil around until his nose was straight. The sound of crunching cartilage was drowned out by his scream.

At the motel, he had just enough energy to pull the ratty-looking bedspread onto the floor before he collapsed into sleep. It was mid-afternoon of the following day when he finally crept around the back of the nursing home. He was counting on the routine the janitor had outlined for him—all the residents would be fed and down for their naps while the staff congregated in the break room to sip coffee and watch the afternoon soaps on TV.

By peeking in the windows he found a mop closet on the same hallway as Viola Nordquist's room and decided to go in that way. Thick metal screens covered all the windows at The Little Sisters but the screws holding them in place were on the outside. They were designed to keep the residents in, not to keep burglars out. Luckily, the screws came out easily; there was hardly any rust. He tried not to hurry, but he was annoyed. A swarm of mosquitoes had found him. He didn't want to make noise by slapping at them, but waving them away did no good. Besides, his nose still ached.

He slipped the catch with his knife, slid the window up, and climbed in. A sliver of light shone on the floor, across the little room. He moved to it and quietly pressed his ear against the door. After several minutes he turned the knob and pushed. The door gave an inch and stopped. It was padlocked on the other side.

TWENTY-FIVE

McKinney woke up early and drove out to Mt. Carmel Cemetery. He parked out on the street and walked in, stepping over the chain across the entrance. The cemetery hadn't officially opened for the day. He gazed out across the graves, looking for the landmark he always used, a tomb with a statue of a soldier on top. The soldier, a man named Onofrio, had died in World War I. McKinney saluted as he walked past him, cutting across the rolling hills of the dead, winding his way between the stones. A light drizzle was falling but he didn't mind. Besides, it was quiet and the slick, newly cut grass smelled fresh and alluring. He sat down next to his wife's grave.

"Catherine," he said, and then fell silent. He wanted to tell her everything. He wanted to tell her that their daughter was turning into a bright and beautiful young woman. He wanted to tell her how strange he'd felt going out with Carla—guilty, but happy. He rubbed the empty ring finger of his left hand. It felt naked.

He lay down across the grave, looking up at the sky, remembering. Once, after a particularly difficult day, he'd come home from work to find a grinning Catherine waiting for him with an old blanket and a picnic basket full of sandwiches. Catherine hadn't been particularly fond of the blues, but she was fond of McKinney. She packed Angelina off to the babysitter's and took McKinney to the Blues Festival in Grant Park telling him, "Relax, dammit, and quit being such a mope." As he lay with his head on her lap, listening to Buddy Guy's wailing guitar, he looked up at her and was overwhelmed. In a rare, poetic moment he told her, "You know, we humans look at birds in flight and think how lucky they are, but the birds don't know they're lucky. Soaring is just their natural state of being. When I'm with you I feel like I'm soaring, and I know how lucky I am."

Mostly, he wanted to tell her about Phillips, about his indecision and his fear of losing his job.

"Only the deluded and the fearful sacrifice truth for comfort," he said. "Your smart-alecky daughter reminded me of that one. She's just like you, a let-tomorrow-take-care-of-itself kind of person. But this isn't just about keeping my job; it's also about keeping my integrity. Forensic scientists have to remain objective. I'm not an advocate for the defense or the prosecution. I'm an advocate for the truth. This kid's being railroaded by a couple of guys who just want to win, and I might be the only one who can help him. The evidence doesn't prove he didn't kill Arnold Drenon and his dogs, but it certainly establishes reasonable doubt. Even if I get to testify, Jameson will probably get the shoeprint evidence from the Burdett case thrown out. Phillips's attorney would have to show relevance. So, here's the conflict—either I recognize my duty to forensic science or my duty to the truth."

When they first started dating Catherine had found a "to do" list McKinney had written. She teased him about it until he tore it up. "Sean, people make lists to have control over their future," she'd said. "The uncertainty makes them nervous. Embrace your uncertainty." Then she'd stuck her tongue in his ear.

His forearm shielded his eyes from the mist. He moved it a little to look up at the gunmetal sky. "You were the most alive person I ever knew," he said. The drizzle was stronger now, not quite rain, but enough to soak his shirt. Wet grass clippings stuck to him as he got up and brushed himself off. He pulled a scrap of paper from his pocket and looked at the phone number for Detective Davis, Boadu's friend out in Aurora. He'd fished it out of the trash, just in case. A trickle ran down his face. "Okay, Catherine," he said, "let's get to work."

The waiting room attached to the ICU at St. Joseph's Hospital was meant to be a pleasant, neutral setting, but the pastel walls and paintings of sunny, flower-filled fields didn't relax McKinney. He'd phoned Boadu's friend, Detective Davis, that morning. They discussed the three murdered seniors, and Davis had agreed the cases were similar, but when McKinney asked him how the investigation into his little old lady was progressing, the answer was disappointing. "I don't really have time to look into this now, McKinney. The family's real upset, and I feel bad for them, but we just don't have much to go on. Our best bet is if the daughter can give us a description, but she's in no shape to answer questions and I'm up to my neck in gang shootings. I'm sorry, I just don't have the time." In addition to killing Gertrude Hoskins, the killer shot her daughter, Marcie, but the woman survived. Now, McKinney sat in an uncomfortable waiting room chair trying to convince Marcie Franklin's husband, John, to let him question her about the attacker. It was turning out to be a hard sell.

"I understand what you're asking," Franklin said, "but I just don't want her to have to relive the whole ordeal. She's not out of the woods yet and answering your questions is bound to upset her."

"I'm not trying to upset her, Mr. Franklin, and I'm sorry to have to impose on you like this, but don't you think she'd want us to catch the man who killed her mother?"

"Look, she was tied to a chair and beaten. She saw the guy murder her mom. Then he shot her in the head. She was in surgery for twelve hours. She's only been conscious for two days, and she's lucky to be alive. I didn't let Detective Davis talk to her, and I'm not letting you talk to her. Not until she gets out of the ICU. The doctors will back me up on that."

"All I want to know is what the attacker asked them. As it is, all we know is that he's attacking older people, seniors. If we find out why, maybe we can prevent the next one."

"My mother-in-law, Gertrude, was just a nice, little old lady. She didn't have anything worth stealing. The guy's probably just looking for old people who have cash squirreled away or something."

McKinney shook his head. "That would make sense if he hadn't left behind cash and jewelry at his other crimes. Did he steal anything from Mrs. Hoskins?"

"I don't know. I haven't been over to her house yet." Franklin's voice quavered slightly. "When I'm not working, I'm here."

McKinney took a good look at the man seated across the table from him—he was stocky, red-faced, and about forty. His hands looked strong, with thick wrists and chapped skin. Franklin appeared to be a man who'd spent time working outdoors. McKinney also noticed the telltale signs of exhaustion. There were sallow bags under his eyes, and the strong hands shook whenever they weren't clenched in his lap. His breath was fetid and his clothes looked like they could stand up on their own. He doubted the man had slept much. McKinney decided to try a different approach. "What if I write my questions down and you take them in to your wife? Your presence won't upset her. You can work the questions into the conversation. If she appears agitated, just stop. If she's willing to talk about it, though, she could save someone's life." McKinney took out a pen and a notebook and jotted down a few questions. He tore out the sheet and pushed it across the table, towards Franklin. "I'll wait right here. Take all the time you need."

Franklin looked at the paper but left it where it lay. He sighed and appeared to shrink a little in his chair. Finally, with an effort, he pushed himself to his feet. He picked up the paper, almost as an afterthought and walked toward the door to the ICU. "I'll try," he said, "but I'm not promising anything."

"Thank you," McKinney said. After Franklin was gone he bought a cup of coffee from the vending machine and settled down to wait. The waiting room was packed, filled with people trying to fend off fear. McKinney looked around. Some huddled together and whispered in low tones. A family in the corner told stories, presumably about their sick relative. One man had almost finished a thick book of crossword puzzles. Most attempted to catch a few minutes of sleep. McKinney remembered the hours he'd spent in a similar room, watching a similar scene. After a while he moved to one of the lounge chairs and leaned back, closing his eyes.

McKinney leans over and studies the lines in his wife's face. He sends her a mental kiss, the mask he's wearing to prevent infection preventing contact. Hers is still a beautiful face, strong, with clean lines at chin and jaw, but now it's thinner, the bone structure obvious. Sepsis has begun to whittle her down. She looks relaxed in sleep, calm, and McKinney is glad. Her body needs the rest. When awake, she struggles to keep from tearing out the respirator.

The morphine/Atavan cocktail they give her makes her delirious. She wants to go home and tries to talk past the tube in her throat. She gets frustrated. McKinney feels an actual, physical pain in his chest when the nurses strap her to the bed with padded restraints. He spends that night with her, propped in the only chair in her little, plastic-walled cubicle. He wakes the next morning, smelling his own sour breath.

He shuffles through the CDs on the small table next to her bed and selects some Native-American flute music, turning the volume low. Sound, he thinks, is the way to touch her. Music to help her relax, to keep her in this world. Music to block the hum of the machines, the steady whoosh of the respirator.

He leaves for a while and, when he returns, he finds that a nurse has turned on the audio for her heart monitor. It's beeping and Catherine is wide eyed, panicky. He imagines her torture, lying there listening to the electronic report of her heart, waiting for it to stop. McKinney yells at the first nurse he sees, not caring that he reduces her to tears.

He scoots the chair closer to her bed and looks out through the clear, plastic wall at the busy nurses' station beyond. He checks the time on her intravenous pumps. They have at least an hour until a nurse will come in to change the bag, an hour alone together. He settles himself in the chair and places his hand next to hers on the bed, the backs of their hands almost touching. He can feel her heat. He closes his eyes.

A hand on his shoulder shook him awake. He looked at his watch. He'd been asleep for three hours. There was a sheen of perspiration on his face and his mouth was dry. John Franklin stood over him.

"Mr. Franklin, I must have dozed off. How's your wife?"

"Stable. I stayed with her until she fell asleep. She answered some of your questions. Once she got started, it sort of flowed out of her. I guess she wanted to talk about it."

"Maybe it comforted her to be able to share it with you."

"Maybe." Franklin pulled up a chair and sat, stroking the stubble on his chin. "I guess there was more to my mother-in-law than I thought. The murderer seemed to think she knew something about a gangster treasure."

"Gangster treasure?"

"Yeah. Back in the 1930s she was in love with a gangster. The guy who attacked Marcie thinks that her gangster was part of a gang that hid some gold coins. He thought Marcie's mom, or one of her friends, could tell him how to find them. She couldn't, so he killed her."

"Gangster gold from the thirties...that's crazy. You said he asked about Mrs. Hoskins's friends. Did she give him the names of any other women?"

"Yeah. I guess she still has one friend from back then, a woman in a nursing home up near St. Paul. Marcie couldn't remember her name, but she told me where her mom keeps her address book. I can take you over there to get it. It would be a shame if some other old lady got killed."

"Thank you, Mr. Franklin. I appreciate all your help." McKinney stood up and stretched his arms over his head, working the kinks out of his back. The two men left the waiting room and headed down the hallway to the parking garage.

As they drove to Aurora, McKinney considered what he should do with this information. Should he call Boadu? Jameson? Anderson? He would definitely call the St. Paul Police Department and ask them to check on the woman in the nursing home. Getting them to stake out her room seemed unlikely, he didn't have enough information to make a convincing argument for that. If there was a chance to catch this guy, though…What kind of a nut tortured old ladies to find missing gangster treasure? It had to be the same guy who'd killed Mr. Drenon. Hell, he'd fly up there and stake out her room himself if he had to. Phillips was innocent and this was his chance to prove it.

He turned to Franklin. "Did your wife say which gangsters are supposed to have hidden this gold? Dillinger? Capone? Pretty Boy Floyd?"

"No. No one she'd ever heard of. The only name she could remember the man saying was Alvin Karpis."

River Bend, Minnesota wasn't in the St. Paul Police Department's jurisdiction. It was in an unincorporated area and a small sheriff's department handled its law enforcement. The deputy McKinney spoke with informed him that they were too busy to go out to the nursing home. McKinney was disappointed but not surprised. He decided to fly up there and talk to the woman, Viola Nordquist. Maybe she would be able to give him some insight into the killer's motive. Gangster gold. Right.

McKinney's mother lived in Minneapolis and McKinney owed her a visit. Angelina could afford to miss a day of summer school. They'd make it a long weekend. He sent Angelina downstairs to ask Carla if she'd take care of Hendrix for a few days while he went online to check fares. As an afterthought, he phoned Detective Boadu.

He recognized Boadu's deep voice. "It's your dime."

"Detective Boadu? This is Sean McKinney. You're showing your age, Detective, phone calls haven't cost a dime since disco was popular."

"McKinney, what's shakin'? My friend Davis, out in Aurora, told me he talked to you. How's my old lady case comin'?"

"That's what I wanted to talk to you about. I think we have three cases linked together now. I spoke to the husband of one of the victims in Davis's case. Apparently our killer is torturing seniors to get information about some gold coins that were squirreled away by gangsters back in the 1930s. Does your victim, Burdett, have any ties to old gangsters?"

"Senior citizen gangsters, huh? You mean like Dillinger, those guys?"

"I guess. Specifically, it was the Barker/Karpis gang but, yeah, like Dillinger. Did you run across any connection like that?"

Boadu chuckled. "Ain't that a kick. No, nothing like that has come up, but I still have a couple of Miss Burdett's relatives to talk to. I'll ask them if she knew any gangsters back in the day."

McKinney decided not to mention his run-in with Detective Barger at Phillips's trial. Apparently Boadu liked him, and he wanted to keep it that way. "Will you let me know if you turn anything up?" he asked.

"You got it, McKinney. And I know you'll do the same for me."

"Absolutely. If I find out anything, I'll let you know."

He hung up the phone and started rummaging through his bedroom closet for an overnight bag.

McKinney didn't like waking in a strange bed, not even the foldout couch in his mother's condo. He was disoriented and not quite sure where he was, in space or time. He briefly looked for Catherine on the other side of the bed, and then he remembered—cancer, the hospital, the funeral. He still wasn't used to waking alone. *You don't get used to losing your wife,* he thought, *you just become functional.*

The sound of clinking silverware woke him the rest of the way, and he heard the rumble of voices from the kitchen, his mother and his daughter. By the time he'd dressed and folded up the sofa bed they had coffee poured and eggs on plates. He slid into his seat at the kitchen table and began spooning sugar into his coffee.

"Mmmm, deluxe service. What did I do to deserve this?"

His mother stood over him, kissed him on the top of the head, and brushed his sandy hair back from his eyes. She was a small woman, with dyed hair that failed to disguise her age. "Not what you did, sweetie. What you're going to do."

His daughter chimed in, "Yeah, Dad. It'll be fun."

"What?" he asked. "What'll be fun?"

His mother smiled and handed him a plate of raisin toast. "Angelina and I want to go to the Raptor Center today."

"And be eaten by dinosaurs? No thanks."

"It's U of M's rehabilitation center for birds of prey."

"Rehab center, eh. What are they addicted to, chihuahuas?"

"C'mon, Dad." Angelina winked at her grandmother. "It's ed-u-cational."

McKinney started to object but his mother gave him The Look. The look that said, *You're doing this, buster, so just shut up and get with the program.* She was famous for The Look, it had worked on him when he was a child, and it had worked on his father.

"Fine," McKinney said, "we can go right after breakfast. You two are on your own tomorrow, though. I've got work to do."

Standing next to a cage containing a one-legged hawk, McKinney and his mother talked while Angelina moved from cage to cage, taking pictures of injured owls and fledgling eagles. McKinney watched his sixteen-year-old daughter and sighed. "She still cries herself to sleep, sometimes."

"It's hard to lose someone you love that much," his mother said. "I know. That's why I moved up here after your father died. Chicago was his town. It was too hard living there by myself. Time will surely help."

"You're right, Mom. And this trip is good for her. She likes coming to visit you."

McKinney's mother put her hand on his arm. "And how are you holding up, honey?"

"Better, I guess. I still think about Catherine all the time but it doesn't immobilize me the way it used to."

"You know, since Angelina taught me to use a computer, we've been corresponding by email. She says that sometimes you just sit, staring, for hours. And sometimes you forget to shave, and you go to work looking rumpled."

"I'll be all right."

She gave his arm a little squeeze. "I know you will, dear. It's Angelina I'm worried about. She needs her father to be strong for her."

"I...you're right, of course." He looked down at his feet. "She probably doesn't feel very secure...taken care of. Truth is, she's usually the one who gets dinner together. I haven't had much of an appetite."

"Look after your child, honey," his mother said. She paused. "And how are things at the crime lab?"

"Okay. I was afraid they were going to fire me for a while. I fell way behind in my casework, had a big backlog. A couple of my cases got nollied."

"Nollied?"

"*Nolle prosequi.* It's Latin. Means the state's attorney had to drop the case. It's one of the cardinal sins of the justice system. I'm all caught up now, though."

"Well, that's good because I have a favor to ask you."

"We're flying back to Chicago day after tomorrow, Mom. I'm just here to interview Mrs. Nordquist."

"I know, but this won't take you very long. I have a friend who's a defense attorney. He has this case...Sean, they've accused a little boy of murdering his sister. He's only ten years old and he's in jail. My friend is his lawyer. He's certain the boy is innocent. I promised him that my son, the forensic scientist, would read the police report and let him know if anything looked odd."

"Mom, I can't—"

"He's just a little boy."

Angelina bounced over from a barn owl's cage. "That bird's name is Whisper. Isn't that cool? What're you guys talking about?"

"Your grandmother is trying to get me to work on my vacation."

"And your father is trying to get out of it."

Angelina hugged her grandmother. "You won, right?"

McKinney's mother gave him The Look. Angelina punched her father on his shoulder. "Ha," she said. "Girl power!"

That evening after dinner McKinney's mother handed him a folder containing reports related to the case of Thomas Jacobs, the ten-year-old charged with murdering his sister. McKinney plopped down on the couch. A breeze coming through the open balcony doors fluttered the pages in the folder as he pored through them.

Thomas Jacobs had gone through a preliminary hearing to determine probable cause for an indictment. Nobody really wanted to indict a ten-year-old child. McKinney had read about the case in the Chicago papers. The boy's twelve-year-old sister, Adele, had been murdered, her body found in a weed-infested, empty lot. Thomas confessed to hitting her with a rock because she wouldn't let him ride her bicycle but claimed he'd run away when she fell.

The first report in the folder was from the medical examiner's office. It listed bruising just above the left temple with minor hemorrhaging underneath, which, along with the boy's confession, was enough for an indictment. The report also listed petechial hemorrhages in the form of pinhead-sized spots around the eyes and a fracture of the hyoid bone in her throat. McKinney thought it likely that she died of strangulation rather than blunt force trauma. Except for a few scratches, some of which had been acquired several days before her murder, the only other physical damage was some contusions on her pelvis. McKinney shuffled through the papers until he found the reports from the crime lab. The lab had failed to find sperm or semen on the vaginal swabs. Pubic combings hadn't contained any hairs that were significantly different from her own.

McKinney turned to the detectives' report. Color copies of some of the crime scene photos were clipped to the front page. He leafed through them. She was a thin child with pale, freckled skin and long, brown hair. She lay on her back, eyes closed, hair fanning out from her head as though it had been arranged that way. She wore a matching blue print skirt and top. The skirt was pulled up around her waist. Her underwear and one brown canvas gym shoe were missing. She wasn't wearing socks. Another photo showed a close up of the missing gym shoe, lying on its side in some weeds. Some pink cloth had been stuffed inside the shoe. McKinney guessed it was the girl's underwear.

He flipped quickly past the photographs to the detectives' report. Their investigation had turned up no witnesses, but they'd speculated on the sequence of events. The girl had been struck in the head with the rock and fallen off her bicycle. While lying dazed on the ground she'd been strangled. Then, her underpants had been ripped off her body, stuffed in her shoe, and the shoe thrown away. After that she'd been raped. There was no suggestion that anyone other than the girl's brother had touched her and there was no explanation offered for the absence of semen. The implication, though, was obvious— since the boy was only ten years old he was physically unable to produce semen.

What, if anything, stood out from the reports? *Strangled? Ripped?* What had the detectives meant by that word? Were the underpants torn off the victim's body or had her attacker slid them down her legs? Was a ten-year-old boy strong enough to tear off someone's underpants? He flipped through the file and found a photo of the boy. Unlikely.

McKinney tossed the folder aside and lay back on the couch, closing his eyes. He'd seen the results of violence before, in person and in photographs. Seeing children who were victims of violence never got any easier. The girl hadn't been too much younger than his daughter. He set the folder down and went out to the kitchen.

"So, what do you think?" his mother asked.

"I don't know, Mom. I can't seem to focus. Thinking about that beautiful little girl having her life stolen from her—it just makes me sad. This is the same thing that happens to me all the time at work, I see the results of violence and start to shut down."

"Sean, honey, even when horrible things happen, the world is filled with beauty. Rain still makes the flowers grow. Birds still sing, and the sun still shines. And you have the honor of seeing one of nature's most beautiful shows, a child growing into young adulthood. You just need to start looking again."

McKinney walked to the balcony doors and peered out. The sun was below the horizon but the sky was still bright enough to draw purple shadows on the ground. Minnesota trees were just starting to shed their leaves, and he watched a scattering of them swirl up the side of the building. Down in the yard, Angelina was collecting some of the red and yellow leaves. He called to her, and she looked up and waved.

TWENTY-SIX

The end of 1934 was a happy time for Delroy. His job at the bus station paid just enough for them to have a nice Christmas. Lucille cooked up a burgoo and cornbread that lasted them all week, and a sweet potato pie, made with brown sugar like his mother's. He spent a whole afternoon shopping in the Loop until he found just the right gift for Lucille, a powder blue dressing gown with a sash at the waist. There was even enough to start picking up a few things for the baby. Lucille was starting to show, and Delroy couldn't help but bring home little toys and dolls. Finally, she began to scold him for his extravagance. "Honey, you have got to stop," she would say. "This baby isn't gonna play with all that stuff." But Delroy knew she didn't mean it. Every time he brought home some trinket she would beam at him, and he would think the world was a pretty good place, after all.

In January of 1935 things got even better. The FBI was hot on the trail of the Barker/Karpis gang for the kidnapping of Edward Bremer. The Barkers hadn't bothered Delroy and Lucille in months, but knowing that they were still out there somewhere made them nervous. Though he never mentioned it, the dreadful potential of the Barkers' return hung over Delroy—a blemish on their happiness. On the ninth of that month they read in the paper that Doc Barker and Monty Bolton had been arrested in raids on their north side apartments and, a week later, they heard through Mrs. Finch that the feds had killed Ma and Freddie in Florida. Ziegler had been gunned down in Cicero the year before, so the only one left who knew them was Alvin Karpis. One evening, in the last week of January, Lucille showed Delroy a headline in the *Tribune* saying that Karpis had narrowly escaped capture in Atlantic City. Karpis wasn't in Chicago, thank goodness. Delroy tuned in the *National Barn Dance* on the radio so they could celebrate.

"You don't suppose any of that kidnap money is still down there in Florida?" he asked, as he sashayed Lucille around the kitchenette to "The Wildwood Flower."

"Unless those G-men kept it for themselves, I wouldn't be a bit surprised," she said. "There was never any mention of it in the papers."

"What if you and me go down there and have a look? I know the place Freddie and his Ma were at. He talked about it all the time."

Lucille stopped dancing and looked up at her husband. "I don't know, Dell. What about your job? And what if we run into Karpis or some other gangsters? We're finally getting by and I just don't see that it's worth it."

"I'm not going to quit my job. In fact, that's why we can go. They'll give me a few days off and we can ride the bus for free. As for Karpis, heck, that boy's too busy dodging the law to be hunting Freddie's money. Besides, we could use the money for the baby."

"I'm not sayin' yes but, if we *do* go, what makes you think you can find that money if the feds couldn't? It sounds to me like we're chasin' a greased hog."

"I was around Freddie enough, I know his mind. I bet there's not more than a half dozen places he would have stashed that money." Looking into Lucille's eyes he could see her weakening. "I tell you what, honey…we'll just spend one day down there. With the bus ride there and back, that's about all the time they'll let me have away from work anyway."

"And if we don't find it in one day we'll come right back home?"

Delroy grinned. "I knew you'd say yes." The radio began playing "Keep on the Sunny Side," and he danced her around the room again, covering her upturned face in kisses as they went.

TWENTY-SEVEN

Gilbert swore under his breath at the locked closet door, then climbed back outside and moved down the row of windows to the one he thought was Viola's. The room was dark but through the window he could see the outline of a woman in bed. He removed the screen, slipped the lock and slowly raised the window. It didn't creak. He climbed in and crossed to the door. Again, there was no noise from the hallway. He looked around the room, straining to see in the gloom. The room was neat but drab and not particularly clean. It smelled moldy. There was none of the disinfectant smell he associated with hospitals. A whiteboard over the bed was decorated with cartoon flowers and large, printed letters that read, *My name is Viola—My doctor is Dr. Peters—I am allergic to penicillin.* There was a thin tube coming from the wall that hooked behind her ears and ran under her nose. Terrell had been right.

Gilbert started with the small chest of drawers next to her bed. He slowly pulled out one drawer after another, rifling through underwear, socks, and prayer books. In the bottom drawer he found a small address book and a stack of greeting cards. *All these old ladies like to send each other cards,* he thought. He pocketed the cards and address book and turned to Viola. The woman was unbelievably thin. She slept with her mouth open and her teeth out, a snoring skeleton in a powder blue nightgown. He lowered the rails on both sides of her bed and slid the covers off her. Gathering up the corners of the bottom sheet, he wrapped them around her narrow frame. It was a flat sheet. Unlike a fitted sheet, the nursing home could use it on the top or bottom. *Cheap bastards*, he thought. He tied the sheet tight around her, just as she was waking up. He peeled the oxygen tube off, picked her up and carried her to the open window. She started to mutter questions at him as he boosted her out the window, feet first.

He was leaning out of the window, gripping the sheet and lowering her to the ground, when he heard the door open behind him. The overhead fluorescents flickered on. A nurse in purple scrubs stood in the open doorway. Gilbert let go of the sheet and Viola dropped the remaining two feet to the ground. He thrust his hand into his pocket but couldn't find the Beretta. He'd inadvertently stuffed Viola's address book in the same pocket, and it was on top of the gun, blocking it.

TWENTY-EIGHT

McKinney had dropped his mother and daughter at a shopping mall before driving out to The Little Sisters nursing home. Once there, he'd followed a nurse down a long, beige-tiled hallway to one of the resident rooms. The walls and floor looked grimy to him, and the place had a pervasive odor that he couldn't quite identify. He thought it smelled a little like garden mulch. Whatever it was smelled funky.

He was behind the nurse when she opened the door and snapped on the light, so he couldn't immediately see what in the room had made her gasp. He craned his head forward and saw an empty bed and a man standing by an open window. The man was dressed all in black, wore combat boots, and carried a little flashlight in one hand. He was squinting at them, as though the overhead light hurt his eyes, and that, combined with his disheveled hair and sweat-glistened face, gave him a mad, dangerous look. McKinney pulled his cell phone from his pocket, punched in 911, then quickly handed the phone to the startled nurse. The man started to climb out the window, but McKinney rushed across the room and caught his leg before he could get all the way through. The man kicked backward, catching McKinney in the stomach, but he kept his grip on the man's leg, pulling him back into the room. An uppercut caught McKinney on the cheek, knocking him to the floor. *This is the killer*, he thought. *The man Detective Boadu wants, the man whose capture could free John Phillips.* McKinney would bet on it, and he wasn't letting go. He braced his feet against the baseboard and twisted the trapped leg. The man grabbed the windowsill to steady himself and kicked again. This time he caught McKinney square in the solar plexus. The blow shocked his diaphragm, making it impossible to breathe. He tried to pull air into his lungs, but nothing happened. His chest didn't move. His mouth opened wide, but he made no noise. His hands grew weak. With one desperate pull the killer freed his leg and hurled himself through the window.

Finally, with a gasp, McKinney's lungs began pumping again. As he lay there, gulping in air, he heard Viola Nordquist cursing and swearing, a sheet-wrapped mummy, lying under her bedroom window. He heard the killer's own obscenities echoing back to join Viola's in a profane chorus as he left her there and ran off into the woods behind the nursing home.

McKinney got up from the floor, massaging his swelling cheek. He went outside with the nurse and the newly arrived deputy sheriff and helped them bring Viola back inside. She was upset and confused but unhurt. The deputy went back outside to look for Viola's attacker, and the nurse gave her a sedative. As she relaxed, the lines in her face deepened, turning it mask-like. The nurse left to answer a call, and McKinney looked around the sparsely furnished room. The walls were painted an institutional green that bordered on brown under the fluorescent light. The floor tiles were gray, drab and scuffed. McKinney looked down at Viola and, without knowing why, felt ashamed. He tried to imagine what it must be like to be old and frightened, spending your last days in a place like this. The nurse had told him that Viola had no family. She would die here, alone. He took the old woman's hand, stroking its parchment-thin skin and sat with her while she softly cried herself to sleep.

The next morning, McKinney sat talking with his mother over coffee and painkillers. He ate his blueberry muffin while pressing an ice pack against his cheek.

"Call your defense attorney friend," he said, "and tell him to pay attention to the girl's underpants. Tell him to find out if they're torn and if the forensic biology unit at the crime lab checked them for stains. If they haven't, they need to."

His mother grabbed a pencil and scribbled down the instructions.

McKinney spent the rest of the morning in a funk. He was stretched out on the couch, watching a TV courtroom show, when his mother came in from the kitchen and switched off the television.

"Hey, I was watching that. A woman was suing her landlord to get her security deposit back, but all the judge wanted to hear about was why she installed a stripper pole in the living room—"

She ignored him. "Why don't you quit moping around and take us all to lunch?"

"I'm sorry, Mom. I'm just not very good company today. How about if I take us all out for dinner before we go to the airport?"

"You need to get off your rump, honey."

Angelina scurried in, interrupting. "So, what are we doing about lunch? I'll cook if you want. I've got lots of good recipes." She looked at her father. "Can you take me to the store?"

"Why don't you see what I've got in the kitchen, first," her grandmother said. "Tell me what you need and I'll tell you if I've got it. Besides, your father might not want to go to the grocery store. He might be embarrassed." She winked at Angelina.

"Oh, Mom," McKinney said. He took the ice pack off his

cheek and touched the cool skin. "Not this story again."

"It seems," she said, taking Angelina's hand, "that when you were a very little girl, you occasionally threw temper tantrums. One time, when you and your mom and dad were at the grocery store, you lay down on the floor and started screaming and kicking your feet because they wouldn't buy you any candy. Well, your mother was always full of creative solutions. She lay down next to you and started screaming and kicking her feet, too. You were so surprised you stopped crying and sat right up."

"And I was so embarrassed I moved back about twenty feet to watch," McKinney said.

"Your mother took advantage of your dad's bashfulness. She picked you up and followed him around the store saying things like, 'Please darling, don't throw us out into the cold,' and, 'Deny us if you will, Clarence, the child is yours.' Your mother had a marvelous sense of humor."

Angelina threw her head back and laughed. She laughed until her sides hurt. She wiped away tears that were equal parts joy and sorrow. "Ha!" she said. "Mom owned you, Dad."

McKinney smiled. "Yes," he said. "Yes, she did."

They got back from St. Paul on Sunday evening. Angelina picked up Hendrix from Carla's apartment and took him for a walk while McKinney phoned his voice mail at the lab and listened to the messages. There was one from Boadu. "Hey, McKinney. I looked into that business about the old gangsters. Turns out my victim's older sister was tight with a guy named Harry Campbell, a member of that Barker gang. Sounds crazy but maybe that's what connects these murders after all."

McKinney flipped open his laptop and navigated to the

FBI's website. In their Freedom of Information Act electronic reading room he found a lengthy document about the Barker/ Karpis gang. Between that and an hour's worth of Internet searches he had what sounded like plausible links for all the murders, plausible but crazy. The first victim, Arnold Drenon, had been the brother of Freddie Barker's girlfriend. Florence Burdett was the sister of Wynona Burdett who had been the girlfriend of another gang member, Harry Campbell. Gertrude Hoskins' killer had questioned her about the Barker gang, and Gertrude had given him Viola Nordquist's name. McKinney opened the M.E.'s file on Lefty Egan. Egan had been in Alcatraz, and so had several of the members of the Barker/ Karpis gang. Gangster gold? Ma Barker? All far-fetched but plausible.

He wandered out to the kitchen, made himself a cheese sandwich and an iced tea and sat down at the kitchen table. He nibbled the sandwich for a while, finally giving up and handing the rest to the dog. Hendrix happily trotted out to the living room with the remains and demolished them on the Persian rug. McKinney was not happy. Neither the River Bend Sheriff's Department nor the St. Paul police had been able to track down the man who'd broken into the nursing home. He phoned Carla. There was no answer, so he went downstairs, picked a flower from the backyard garden and propped it up against her door with a little card that said, "Thank you."

On Monday there was a note taped to McKinney's door when he got home from work. It read simply, "Come downstairs." McKinney went downstairs to knock on Carla's door but it was already open. She stood there, leaning against the doorjamb and smiling.

"Okay, I forgive you," she said.

"You forgive me? But I didn't..."

"I would think you would have learned by now that when you're dealing with a woman, it doesn't matter if you're right or wrong. Forgiveness is the best you can hope for."

"Well, if that's your final offer, but I'm not making a dime on it."

She stepped closer to McKinney and lightly touched the ugly, purple bruise on his cheek. "What happened here?"

"Got punched." He kissed her just as Mrs. Vladic came up from the landing below.

"Hey, get a room you two," she said.

Carla winked at her. "Excellent suggestion." She pulled McKinney into her apartment and closed the door.

McKinney felt suddenly self-conscious. He put his hands in his pockets and wandered around the living room, commenting on the profusion of pictures that covered the walls.

Carla placed a hand on his chest and gave him a gentle shove toward the couch. "Sit," she ordered. "I'll nuke us some coffee."

Ten minutes later they were seated at opposite ends of the couch, Carla leaning back against a bolster, her legs folded beneath her and McKinney hiding behind his coffee cup. "Good coffee," he said. He immediately regretted his retreat into small talk. "I'm sorry. That was cowardly."

"No, no…I'm nervous too." Carla stared down into her cup. "Maybe we should have had sex on our first date. I mean, that's not something I ever do, but then we'd be past worrying about it. It wouldn't be another presence in the room."

McKinney crossed, and then uncrossed, his legs. "I'm not sure that would've helped. We've got other issues to work out."

"When I was in college, a boy I liked, but barely knew, approached me at a party and asked if I wanted to help him try out his new waterbed. I was insulted that he thought I was that easy. I turned him down, but I've always felt that I may have missed an opportunity to get to know him."

"He sounds like kind of a jerk. Maybe you're better off."

"Maybe. Beyond making babies, I think of sex as a way for people who care for one another to communicate. I don't want to look back on this as a missed opportunity, Sean. Not for sex, but to really get to know you."

"What about my emotional availability?"

"Yeah." Carla grinned and shook her head. "Sorry about that. I guess I've got some residual trust issues from a couple of disappointing relationships. I'll deal with it."

An ambulance sped past on the street below, its siren drawing attention to the quiet in the room. Carla went to the stereo and put on a CD. The room filled with Aretha's gritty-smooth voice belting out "Chain of Fools."

McKinney leaned back against a cushion and closed his eyes. He realized he was feeling something he hadn't felt in quite a while, a sense of expectation. He had tried hard not to think about the future since Catherine's death. Now, today, he was experiencing an inkling of possibility.

An hour later they were sitting naked on Carla's bed, eating peanut butter out of the jar with spoons, and blackberries from a big plastic bowl. McKinney scooped up a blob of peanut butter and topped it with a berry. He decided it was delicious in the same way as a marshmallow toasted over a campfire. It was the occasion that made it so. He stuck the spoon back in the jar, then laced his fingers behind his head and lay back on the pillows. The setting sun filled the room with a pale, orange light. A half dozen unfinished statues threw indigo shadows across the room as they encircled the bed like a silent Greek chorus.

"These are my muses," Carla said. She pointed to the nearest statue and worked her way around the room. "This is Melina Mercouri, Rosa Parks, Frieda Kahlo, Mary Cassatt, Simone de Beauvoir and, of course, Mrs. Emma Peel. They've all helped me out when I was feeling puny or uninspired."

McKinney placed his hand on Carla's waist. Of all the bits of anatomy that are unique to a woman, this curve was McKinney's favorite. The gentle geometry of waist blossoming into hips felt like the place that nature had always intended his hand to rest. He looked up and saw Carla watching him. "This is nice," he said.

Carla held up a blackberry between her thumb and forefinger. "Open." McKinney opened his mouth. The berry bounced off his nose and rolled off the bed. It stopped to rest against Mrs. Peel's foot.

"The other night...before we argued," McKinney said, "you asked me about Catherine. I want to tell you something about her."

"You don't have to, I understand."

"No, I want to." He rotated his hand in a motion that encompassed the bedroom. "This is a big deal for me...sex, I mean. I haven't slept with anyone since Catherine. Not because I haven't wanted to have sex, but because I didn't want to talk to anyone in bed. Talking in bed is different. You say things that you would never say anywhere else. Intimacy isn't really about sex, it's a way of showing someone you trust them. It's like when a dog rolls onto its back and exposes its throat."

"There's a nice image. So, you trust me not to rip out your jugular?"

"Maybe. No, I think what I'm saying is, I want to trust you."

"Okay," she said, "that's something."

"After Catherine was gone, and I was through dealing with the doctors and the funeral home and everything had settled down, I realized that I hadn't cried. I missed her more than I ever imagined I could miss anyone, but I couldn't cry." McKinney took a breath. "I couldn't cry, because I hated her. I hated her for leaving us, for leaving me to raise our teenage daughter by myself. I didn't want the sole responsibility for her life. It's too much. Anyway, I couldn't talk to anyone about it. I certainly couldn't tell Angelina." He looked down at his feet. He couldn't look at Carla. The truth about his feelings disgusted him. He didn't want to see disgust or worse, pity, on her face. "I felt like a clenched fist. I was angry all the time. I stopped seeing people. I stopped answering the phone. Whenever I walked anywhere I punched street signs and parking meters. One time a cop yelled at me for punching a No Parking sign."

Carla put her hand on McKinney's forehead and pushed his head back so she could see his eyes. "Thank you for telling me," she said.

"Sure, sure," he said, taking her hand off his forehead and holding it gently. "So, tell me about the Sunday afternoon gardening club."

Carla grabbed a handful of blackberries. "We call ourselves the Cubbies Garden Club because Mrs. Vladic is such a huge Cubs fan. She's the real brains of the operation. When Vishal and I said we were interested in growing some vegetables, she went out and bought us trowels, gardening smocks, and Cubs hats. She knows a lot about planting and soil conditions and garden pests. She grew up on a farm in the Balkans."

"Vishal wears a smock?"

"I don't think he wants to, but Mrs. Vladic looked hurt whenever one of us came out without one on, so now we all wear the smocks. Angelina wears a smock."

"I didn't even know she had a smock."

"Oh, yeah, she digs the smock. We all love having her garden with us. She's really a bright girl. Vishal likes to tell her stories about growing up in India. He seems to think they're instructive or inspirational, but usually they're just pointless."

"Like what?" McKinney asked.

"Well, the most recent story was about his grandfather. Vishal's family moved to America because of the caste system in India. They were lower caste and lived in a village surrounded by small farms. His grandfather's goat got loose once and ate some of the neighbor's crops, so the neighbor killed the goat. When his grandfather confronted him, the neighbor denied it. Vishal's grandfather filed charges, and the village judge decided to question the neighbor using the hot knife test."

"What the hell is the hot knife test?"

"You heat up a knife in a fire and touch it to the person's leg. If they're guilty it burns them, but if they're innocent it won't hurt them at all."

McKinney scooped a glob of peanut butter out of the jar. "When was this, the Middle Ages?"

"No. When Vishal was a teenager. Anyway, as soon as the hot knife got near the man's leg he confessed."

"Of course he confessed. Who the hell wouldn't? Reminds me of a case I'm working on now. This autistic guy confessed to murdering an old man, but I don't think he's the killer. I can't prove that he didn't do it, but I don't think he did. That's why I flew up to St. Paul last week. I may have actually seen the real killer. He was trying to kidnap an old lady from a nursing home. I had him." His voice faded. "I had him, and I let him get away."

McKinney told her the whole story—about Phillips, and Anderson, and Boadu. About his work on the evidence and what he thought it meant. When he got to the part about the Minnesota nursing home she kissed his bruised cheek.

"I thought you just worked in the lab. The idea of you chasing after killers frightens me."

"I don't plan on making a habit of it. If I ever see this guy again it'll be in court."

"Think they'll catch him?"

"Maybe. Angelina and I are supposed to go to Florida for a few days after she finishes summer school, but I'd rather stay here in case they pick him up. It's my grandmother's ninety-fifth birthday though."

"Ninety-five? You should definitely go."

"I know... Want to come with us?"

"Maybe." She leaned over and kissed him on the mouth. It was a kiss that turned her "maybe" into a "yes." McKinney spooned a dollop of peanut butter onto her left breast.

"Hey, you got peanut butter on my boob."

McKinney grinned. "You got boob in my peanut butter."

TWENTY-NINE

The bus ride from Chicago to Florida had been a slow striptease. Even though it was the middle of winter there was a good sixty degrees difference in temperature between the two places. They left wearing overcoats, gloves, and galoshes but, by the time they arrived, Delroy was down to his undershirt. Lucille's pregnant body made the last two hundred miles sticky and uncomfortable for her. Still, neither complained. They were hot and tired, but they were on an adventure, and they were together.

Lake Weir was right in the middle of the state, almost equidistant between the gulf and ocean. To be on the safe side, they stopped at Ocala and took a room at a little motor hotel out on Maricamp Road, the misnamed Gulf Breeze. Delroy noted that the only breeze was coming in off the swamp, and it smelled like rotting vegetation and dead fish. Lucille reluctantly agreed to stay in the room. The heat and the bouncing bus trip had drained her energy. Delroy hired an old Model A Ford pickup from the hotel owner and drove the final twenty miles south to Lake Weir alone.

The first four lake access roads he tried led to fishing camps, only one of which was being used. Delroy slammed the truck into reverse and backed out as soon as he saw the fishermen sitting on the little pier. He didn't want to be seen, and the idea of running into one of Freddie's pals made him jumpy. Fortunately, the area was lush with vegetation. Trees lined the rutted roads, and the Spanish moss hung low, giving him cover from the men on the lake. The fifth road dead-ended at what was left of a cottage. All the windows were broken out, and the front was riddled with bullet holes.

Delroy turned the truck around in the sandy furrows that passed for a road and parked it facing out, in case he needed to leave in a hurry. He walked clear around the house once, peering in the windows to be certain he was alone. The front door had been blasted off its hinges, but someone had set it back in the door frame. Delroy gave it a little push and winced at the noise it made when it fell inward, onto the floor. He stepped past the door and entered the grim dwelling that told the story of the Barkers' last hours.

The floors were covered with shards of glass, chunks of plaster, and loose stuffing from the furniture. The walls were decorated with the patterns left by thousands of bullets, from small pockmarks to gaping holes, and there were empty shell casings everywhere. Near the windows, a few had embedded themselves in the walls, after being ejected at high speed from Freddie's Tommy gun. Delroy pulled the square-headed nail out of his pocket and used it to dig one of the shells out of the plaster. It was a big .45 caliber.

Practically every square foot of the house was perforated. Delroy followed the bullet holes up the small staircase to an upstairs bedroom. There he saw the brown spatters and smears left by Ma and Freddie's blood. A jagged piece of glass on the floor caught his attention. It was leaning against the wall, where it had fallen, and Delroy could see himself in the glass. Thinking it was part of a mirror he picked it up and examined it. It was window glass, but one side was covered with a spray of blood. Staring at the distorted reflection of his face gave Delroy a chill. If he'd stuck with Freddie he and Lucille could have been blown apart by bullets in that room. He tossed the glass out the broken window and shuddered. His gaze followed the arc of the glass, out the window to the lake beyond. A man was walking along the shore toward the house. Beyond him Delroy could see a small dock and a dilapidated boathouse under a tree. He started to pull back from the window, but the man was waving. He had already seen him. Delroy waved back, then turned and hurried down the stairs to meet him outside. As he approached, Delroy saw that he was a black man, probably in his forties, with short-cropped hair. His shirt looked like it might have been white once but was now yellowed and stained by years of wear. The man's trousers were held up with a rope, knotted around his waist. Delroy waved again.

"How y'all doin'?" he shouted. He made an effort to banish any hint of the nasal twang he'd picked up in Chicago. He wanted the man to think he was a local.

"Fine," the man answered. "Mighty fine. How you?"

Delroy walked out to meet him. "Live around here?" he asked. He extended his hand. The black man looked at it for a second, then shook it and grinned. The grin exposed a gap where several teeth had been.

"Yasuh, 'cross the lake. But I'm thinkin' y'all are from somewhere else. White folk 'round here don't offer to shake my hand much."

Delroy grimaced. He hadn't thought of that. "Kentucky," he said.

"Well, welcome to the sunshine state. Name's Willie. I take care of this place. What there is left of it, anyway. You come to see where the kidnappers got killed?"

"Yeah, I was just passin' through. Figured I'd take a look."

"I was here when it happened. In fact, I was the first one seen 'em dead. The cops sent me in after they finished shootin' the place up. They figured them Barkers wouldn't kill me 'cause I helped 'em with the boat and all. They was both lyin' on the floor and covered with blood." They started toward the house. "I ain't been back since, but I was hopin' one of them guns was still here. They had a whole lot of guns, and I could sure use one for huntin'. Maybe get us some possum or squirrel once in a while. I don't make much money, and it seems like with kids, the bigger they get, the more they eat."

"Yeah, that's about right," Delroy said. They walked up into the house. Delroy went to the little kitchen, and Willie followed him. "Is this water any good?" Delroy turned the tap and watched the running water go from rust-colored to light ochre. It smelled like sulfur.

"Tastes a mite swampy," Willie said. "But it won't kill you. We're used to it 'round here."

Delroy cupped his hand under the stream and took a sip. He spat it into the sink. How was he going to hunt for the money with this man tagging along behind him? He doubted there were any guns left behind. The feds would have made a thorough search, but it would take time to convince Willie of that, and he didn't have much time left. The shadows outside were getting longer. He looked the black man in the eye and made a decision. "Willie, I'm gonna level with you. I'm looking for the kidnap money. I figure the Barkers must have hid their share out here somewheres, and I aim to find it. If you help me I'll split it with you, fifty-fifty." He stuck out his hand again. The other man shook it with even more enthusiasm.

"I'm mighty glad to hear you say that, mister. That's what I'm lookin' for, too. I didn't really figure there was any guns left 'round here." He stepped out onto the back porch and came back with a shovel and a length of metal pipe. "Let's get to lookin'."

They worked with the ferocity and speed of men who knew

they had been given an opportunity that wouldn't last. Soon, more treasure hunters would show up, and the gawkers and the rubes'd be right behind, hoping to get a peek at the place where the Barkers made their last stand. Sweat soaked their shirts and dripped off their chins as they pried up floorboards and tore holes in the walls. Delroy soaked his handkerchief in the foul-smelling water and knotted it around his forehead. As dusk settled in they moved outside, digging anywhere the ground looked like it had been disturbed. A swarm of mosquitoes attacked briefly, but a wind from the lake carried them away before they could do much damage. Finally, it was too dark to see. The sun was down and the moon hadn't risen yet. They went back into the house and Delroy choked down some of the water from the tap.

"Well," he said. "I reckon that's about it."

"Nosuh," Willie said. "We got one other place." He opened a cabinet over the sink and pulled out a box of candles and a hurricane lantern. "We got to check the boathouse." He lit one of the candles, placed it on the stand, and fitted the glass chimney over it. The glow gave the demolished kitchen an eerie look, like a battlefield where plates and glasses and flatware were the fallen soldiers. Delroy wetted his handkerchief again in the sink and wiped at the sweat and grime on his neck. He forced a tired smile and said, "Let's go, then." The two men wound their way through the trees and brush to the lake, enveloped in a sphere of candlelight.

THIRTY

Gilbert had been sitting in the little Interstate 40 motel restaurant so long that he barely noticed the haze of smoke and kitchen grease in the air. Bright fluorescent overheads shone on the papers spread across the yellowed, flecked Formica table in front of him. He checked and double-checked the information he'd taken from Viola Nordquist's room, and he was convinced that he was on the right track. There were several letters from a woman living in Ocala, Florida, close to Lake Weir. In one of the letters she even mentioned "Old Creepy." That had to be a reference to Karpis. There were no envelopes, but she was listed in Viola's address book. There were other women in Viola's book, but this had to be the one. He could feel it.

Gilbert gently fingered the bandage across the bridge of his nose as he pored over his maps. He had underestimated the janitor. That wouldn't happen again. He would spend more time with his interviewees, too. He'd analyzed his interrogation of the other old folks and decided that he'd been too hasty. He needed to wring every last drop of information out of these people, and if it took him a couple of days to do it that was okay with him. Besides, this might be the last one alive. If talking to her didn't turn something up, he was out of ideas.

Right now, though, Gilbert's empty coffee cup was pissing him off. It had been empty for twenty minutes, and for ten of those minutes the waitress had been sitting in the last booth, smoking cigarettes and yakking on her cell phone. The last thing he wanted was to draw attention to himself, but he'd run out of patience. He went behind the counter and picked up the coffee pot. The waitress stubbed out her cigarette.

"Hey, mister, only authorized personnel allowed behind the counter."

Gilbert stared down at the hand that gripped the coffee pot and watched his knuckles turn white. He would have enjoyed splashing the scalding liquid in the lazy bitch's face but he knew that would be a mistake. He fought for control and won. He struggled to get one of his practiced smiles working, then turned to face the waitress.

"I'm just trying to help out," he said. "You've probably been on your feet all day. I just thought you could use a little break. Why look here, your cup's empty too." He brought the coffee pot around the counter to where the waitress sat, picking up his own empty cup on the way. He filled both and sat across from her in the booth.

"Ain't you the gentleman." She slipped her cell phone into her purse and shook another cigarette out of the pack. "You must not be from around here. Men in this town are mostly pigs."

He picked up the lighter from the table and held the flame under her waiting cigarette. She looked like she was in her late thirties, a little older than he usually liked, and her two-tone hair made her head look like a sandwich cookie, but she had a nice rack on her.

"My mother taught me manners, that's all. I'm just passing through. Staying right here at the inn, room 209."

"Maybe I was wrong about you being a gentleman, lover. What makes you think I'm interested in your room number?"

He watched her body language as she spoke. On the word "lover" she leaned forward just enough to give him a view of her cleavage. Now he had to figure her game—love or money. He broadened his smile. "I didn't mean anything by it. I'm just a guy passing through with a pocket full of bonus money and nobody to spend it with. I don't even know where to go to pick up a bottle. I thought maybe you'd take pity on a lonely guy and spend a little time with me, that's all."

"Where you passing through to, honey? You on your way to Dollywood?"

Gilbert grinned and smoothed his wavy hair back with his fingers. "Well, yee-fuckin'-ha. Do I look like a hillbilly to you?"

"Didn't mean nothin' by it. Just that most folks that stop here are either goin' to Dollywood or over to the Chattahoochee."

"Nope, I'm going to Raleigh on business. I'm sort of a traveling salesman. What time did you say you were getting off work?"

"Salesman, huh? You're tryin' to sell me something, all right. I get off work in half an hour, but I need to run home and get freshened up. How about I pick you up around nine-ish and we go for drinks? There's a little club I know that stays open late."

Gilbert flashed her his best smile and stood up. "That'll be great. I'm going to go grab a little nap. I've been driving all day. Don't forget, room—"

"I know, sugar. Two-oh-nine."

It turned out that her name was Deidre, and she liked to be on top. She finally showed up at ten with a bottle of cranberry vodka and no need to go out. All this was just fine with Gilbert, though it irritated him that he hadn't gotten her name off her badge at the restaurant; details shouldn't be overlooked. He peeled the cellophane off two motel glasses, poured a couple of good-sized drinks and settled himself in the only chair in the room, leaving her the bed. He let her talk about herself for a while, paying enough attention to nod and "hmmm" in the right places. Finally, she gave him the cue he was looking for, and he moved over to join her on the bed.

She insisted on having the television on. The noise, she said, relaxed her. At first he thought it would be distracting, but he was mesmerized by her pendulous breasts bouncing in front of his face, and the sound of the television soon faded to a distant hum. As he usually did, he catalogued his sensations. It was easier with this one than it had been with some because she didn't expect him to do much. As long as he maintained his erection she was perfectly happy to do the rest. He looked up at her face. She was saying something, though he didn't think she was speaking to him because she was looking up at the ceiling. He liked the ones that talked, as long as he didn't have to answer.

Afterward, she curled up against him and went to sleep. He watched an infomercial for an exercise machine, then slid out of bed to use the bathroom. On the way back to bed he slipped the Beretta out of his pants pocket and sat down in the chair. While she slept he aimed the little gun at her and imagined what it would feel like to pull the trigger. *It would*, he thought, *be a little sad*. Maybe he would enjoy it at first. He would probably enjoy it more than shooting little old ladies. Still, it didn't seem right to kill someone he'd fucked...kind of unappreciative. He put the gun away, pulled on his pants and shook her awake.

"C'mon, baby. Time for you to get up and out."

She was groggy and sat up rubbing her eyes. "Whassa matter, sugar? What time is it?"

"Time for you to go, sugar. Vamoose. Shake a leg." He tossed her clothes onto the bed. She bent over and looked at the clock on the nightstand.

"It's the middle of the night. What the hell's wrong with you?"

"I've got a long drive tomorrow, and I need my sleep. Get dressed and get gone."

It took her less than thirty seconds to dress. He heard the "Fuck" but the slamming door muffled the "you!"

THIRTY-ONE

It was a busy week for McKinney. On Friday, Vivian Washington brought him the evidence from the murder of Gertrude Hoskins and the attempted murder of her daughter. He set everything else aside and took a cursory look through the contents of the big plastic bag. He was disappointed not to find any shoeprints. There was plenty of other evidence to examine, though. Some overly zealous crime scene techs out in Aurora had used a vacuum, gathering trace materials from every room of the victim's house into filter-lined plastic dishes. Most of it would be useless debris, but McKinney would have to go through each dish carefully, and there were dozens of dishes.

Since none of the evidence had come from a suspect he took the whole bag into a clean room and sorted through it. He used a low power stereoscope to pick hairs and fibers off the electrical cords that had bound the victims to their chairs. He placed the cords and the two resulting boxes of trace materials into a separate bag. After changing the white paper on the table, he took a metal spatula and began scraping down the victims' clothing, examining each piece under the stereoscope before packing it away. Later, the clothing would go to the Biology Unit for examination of the stains he'd found. There were also a number of promising-looking hairs, which he placed in a plastic pillbox and labeled "unknowns." He had been given hair standards from the two victims, and he was pretty sure that the unknown hairs hadn't come from either of them. Without a suspect's hair to compare them to they weren't of much use, but what excited him was the nice follicular root attached to several of the hairs. These hairs could be submitted for DNA analysis.

Hairs without a root were only good for physical comparison, a technique McKinney thought was limited, at best. The most you could reasonably say about a physical comparison of two hairs was that they shared a few similar characteristics. You could never say that the hairs were a match, or that a hair had come from a specific individual, and there were no valid statistics from which to infer a range of probability. Mitochondrial DNA could be extracted from rootless hair, but the procedure was more difficult and the results not as precise as a nuclear DNA comparison.

Around two, hunger got the better of him, and he decided to break for lunch. He packed up the evidence and took it down to the vault. He was putting it on the shelf designated for his cases when Vivian Washington came in.

"I'm glad I found you, McKinney. I want to talk to you."

McKinney smiled. "Hey, Viv. Want to go back to your office?" He pointed to the vault surveillance camera. "We're not really alone."

Vivian put her hand on the door. "Let's talk here."

"Uh, oh. That sounds ominous. What's up?"

Vivian leaned back against one of the shelves and sighed. She buried her hands in the pockets of her lab coat. "I got two phone calls about you today. One was from Moses, telling me how you saved some old lady's life up in Minnesota. He and his friend in Aurora are going to have another talk with Detective Barger because they figure you're right about a connection between the three murders. The other call was from Director Roberts."

"Thanks for telling me about Moses. That's wonderful, but

I guess we're hiding in the evidence vault because of the call from Roberts. What did he want?"

"I don't know, but he told me to send you to his office right away. You must be in a hot mess, this time. He sounded happy." She put her hand on McKinney's shoulder. "Good luck, Sean. If he fires you, I'll be glad to write you a letter of recommendation."

"Thanks, Viv." McKinney opened the vault door and stopped. "If he does can me, will you work the old lady cases for me?"

"Supervisors don't do casework, McKinney. But I'll make sure they're assigned to someone competent." McKinney started down the hall. "He said you're to go straight to his office," Vivian called after him.

There were two state troopers standing outside Director Roberts's office when McKinney got there. He walked past them, through the open door, and stood in front of the director's desk. Stanley Roberts looked up at him. "Ah, there you are. Have a seat." He motioned to a chair with the sheaf of papers in his hand.

McKinney sat. "You wanted to see me?"

"Yes, indeed. McKinney, I have good news and bad news. First the good—I've asked the Department of Internal Investigations to cancel your CADM. There'll be no investigation, and you won't be called in to DII to answer questions."

"Great," McKinney said. "Thanks."

"Now, the bad news. I've been told that you recently mis-represented yourself as a police officer on at least two occasions. You're not a police officer, McKinney. You're a civilian employee, and I believe that I have sufficient justification to fire you. You're fired, McKinney."

"But, that's not true. If you're talking about my going to the nursing home in Minnesota—"

"Yes, and your recent talk with a crime victim's husband at a suburban hospital."

"In both of those instances I only identified myself as an employee of the crime lab."

"And flashed a badge, implying that you were a police officer. That's a crime, McKinney. I could send you to jail."

McKinney stood up and leaned across the massive oak desk separating the two men. "I never flashed a badge! I don't even own a badge. Where did you get that idea?"

Roberts consulted one of the papers in his hand. "A Mr. Franklin called here to verify your employment. He was surprised to learn that you were not working in an official capacity when you showed up at the hospital to question his wife. He said that you showed him some kind of badge."

"I showed him my employee ID card. Like I said, I don't own a badge."

"It's your word against his. Besides, interviewing victims isn't your job. You aren't allowed to do it in any capacity, official or not." Roberts leaned back in his chair and smiled. "And what about your precious objectivity? Acting as both scientist and detective shoots your standing as 'Mr. Forensic Scientist' all to hell, doesn't it? You're through, McKinney. Take off your lab coat and ID and leave them on the chair. These officers will escort you out of the building."

"Don't I get some kind of a hearing?"

"Oh, yeah. According to your union contract you can challenge the firing and have a hearing. Call your union rep." Roberts waggled his hand at McKinney in a dismissive gesture. "Now, get out of my lab."

McKinney struggled to come up with a snappy comeback.

He searched his mind for an insect analogy for Roberts. *A Robber Fly*, he thought, *an insect that stabs its prey, paralyzes it, then sucks out all its bodily fluids—Stanley Robberfly.* He couldn't think of any way to say it that wouldn't make him sound like a truculent schoolboy. Maybe his actions had been immature. He was angry with Roberts for firing him, but he was even angrier with himself. Roberts was right about his lapsed impartiality. Maybe he should have left the investigating to the detectives. His concern for Phillips, and his desire to find the truth, had eclipsed his adherence to the code of his profession. He hoped it hadn't been in vain. At last, all he could mutter was, "What about my stuff? I've got personal items at my desk."

"I'll have your supervisor pack them in a box. You can pick them up at reception tomorrow." Roberts motioned to the troopers waiting outside the door. "Officers, show Mr. McKinney the way out." They entered and stood on either side of McKinney as he stepped away from the director's desk. The two officers were careful not to touch him as, grumbling and red-faced, he started down the hallway to the parking lot exit. He looked back in time to see a smiling Stanley Roberts wiping his handprints off the smooth, shining top of the antique Wooton desk.

When he got home McKinney found Angelina huddled on the couch waiting for him, her sneaker-clad feet resting on a suitcase. He looked around the room. The television was off, and so was the stereo.

"Going somewhere?" he asked.

"Dad, I think we should leave for Great-grandma Lucy's tonight. You can take an extra day off work, can't you?"

He plopped himself down on the couch next to her. "I don't think that'll be a problem. I got fired today."

"Uh, oh. Is it because of that case with the guy who reminds you of a cat?"

"Sort of. It's because I stuck my nose where it didn't belong. Real forensic scientists don't behave like those goofballs on television. My job is to analyze evidence, not solve crimes. I got involved and stopped thinking like a scientist."

Angelina gave his hand a squeeze. "Maybe you were thinking like a person."

"Thanks, kiddo." He gave a snort of self-abasement. "So, what's this all about?" He pointed to her suitcase. "Why do you want to leave tonight? We're not supposed to be at your great-grandmother's for four days. It'll only take us two days to drive down there."

"I don't really know," she said. "I'm just worried about her. Did you know that she and Great-grandpa hung out with gangsters when they lived in Chicago, back in the olden days?"

"I remember my dad teasing her about it at holiday dinners. He'd say stuff like, 'You better finish your potatoes, boy. If your grandma thinks you don't like her cooking she'll take you for a one-way ride.' Then he'd point at me and make a rat-a-tat sound, like a Tommy gun. Why? Are you worried about the guy who killed those old ladies?"

"You said he's torturing women who knew gangsters back then."

"Sure, but he's operating here in the Midwest. It seems unlikely that he'd wind up in Florida."

"But not impossible, right?"

"No, not impossible. Angelina, your great-grandmother's okay, but I don't want you to worry. I'll call Carla and ask her if she can leave a little ahead of schedule. Mrs. Vladic has agreed to take care of Hendrix. You go downstairs and ask if she can start a couple of days earlier."

"I'm on my way," Angelina said. She hopped up and kissed him on the cheek. "Thanks, Dad. You're the best."

"No problem," he said. But she was gone so fast that he said it to the closing door and the fading scent of her too-sweet perfume. McKinney reached for the phone. It rang before he could pick it up.

"McKinney here."

"Well, you must have been sitting right on top of the phone," his mother said.

"Hi, Mom. Yep, and it's darned uncomfortable, too."

"Ha ha. Guess who I just spoke with?"

"I don't know, Aunt Opal?"

"Sean, your Aunt Opal has been dead for eight years. Try to keep up, dear."

"Okay, I give up. Who did you just speak with?"

"My attorney friend, the one defending the little boy accused of killing his sister."

"So, what happened? Was he able to get the underpants analyzed?"

"He was. He has a friend in the prosecutor's office. You were right about them. They were torn clear down one side. The crime lab here used some kind of special light and found a stain on them. It was semen, and the DNA matched a man who lived right behind the empty lot where they found the girl's body. He'd been in jail before, for a sex crime he committed a long time ago, so they had his DNA in some kind of database. He must have been watching the children and saw his chance when the boy ran away. My friend says 'thanks' and he'll buy you dinner the next time you come to visit."

"That's great, Mom. I'm glad it worked out." McKinney smiled. *Finally*, he thought, *I've managed to do something right.*

"Thanks for helping out, honey. And how's my favorite granddaughter?"

"She's fine. I'm taking her to Florida to visit Dad's mother."

"Well, won't that be a treat."

"Come on, Mom. I know you don't like Lucy, but Angelina's crazy about her."

"Alright, honey. I'll mind my manners. And you have as good a time as you can."

THIRTY-TWO

Delroy peered over Willie's shoulder as he pushed the door to the boathouse open and held the lantern in the doorway. It was nothing more than a small pine shed built on a few pilings that had been driven into the lake bottom. The lantern lit up the gray, weathered wood and the dozens of cobwebs. The moon was just coming up, and Delroy could see the shimmering lake water in the spaces between the planks. The wall opposite the door was missing, to allow the boat access to the lake. *On a dark night like this*, Delroy thought, *anyone on the lakeshore could see the lit-up boathouse and know someone's pokin' around.*

He squeezed past Willie and started to search. The walls were bare except for a few life preservers and a pair of oars. The life preservers had been slashed open where they hung. The boat was a long, flat-bottom skiff with an outboard motor at the rear. It was tied to a piling but lay half submerged in the water. Someone had blasted a hole in its side with a shotgun. Willie handed Delroy the lantern and began to lower himself into the water so that he could get a look under the wood slats that passed for the boat's seats. Delroy grabbed his shoulder and held him back.

"Hold up a sec, Willie. Don't you think we ought to check for alligators and such before you go into the water?"

"Thank yuh, mister, but most of 'em are hunkered down in the mud for the night. I'll be fine." He slid the rest of the way in, then held onto the back of the boat, the brackish water slapping against his chest. "This is the boat them Barkers used to hunt down Old Joe."

"Old Joe?"

"Old Joe was the biggest gator in Lake Weir. Mister Freddie heard about him and decided to hunt him. I drove the boat while he trailed a line with a whole pig on the end of it. We had to go real slow 'cause that pig kept riding up on our wake, just like it was swimmin' or somethin'. Anyway, when a gator would come up behind the pig Mister Freddie would pick up that machine gun and start shootin'."

"Did he get Old Joe?"

"Oh, we seen him, alright. Old Joe took that pig down to the bottom and started rollin'. Mister Freddie was mad 'cause he'd missed his shot, so he started pulling on the rope. If Old Joe hadn't come up to the surface I think he would have tipped us in. Anyway, he grabbed the gun and fired the whole drum at that gator. Old Joe went back under, and we never did find him again. I reckon Mister Freddie got him." Willie shook his head. "It's a shame 'cause folks say he was over a hunnerd year old."

"Some people are just full of hate, Willie."

"Yasuh. And Missus Barker was just as bad. She talked like the whole world was rotten and out t' get her. I figure hate's what killed them Barkers."

Delroy replaced the burned-down candle in the lantern with a fresh one and shone the light on the nearest piling. The water was clear enough to see the sandy bottom so he set the lantern down and eased himself in. He gritted his teeth and tried to steel himself against the fear of chomping jaws finding him in the dark. The cool water lapped against his chest, and he held his breath to bend down and feel around the piling. The wood was covered with mussels and weeds, but he didn't feel anything unusual.

"That's a good idea, mister," Willie said. "There are six of them posts. You check those three, and I'll take the three on this side of the boat."

The two men dove again and again, and finally Delroy felt a hard, slick bulk at the base of the deepest piling. He surfaced, sputtering with excitement.

"I think I got something here. But it's fixed down there pretty good, wrapped around with a leather belt or something."

Willie hoisted himself out of the water, then reached into his pocket and pulled out a long folding knife, snapping it open with one hand. The candlelight was flickering in the breeze and it illuminated Willie's gap-toothed grin as he hovered over Delroy. Clinging to the piling, Delroy held the rocking skiff off with one hand. He looked up into the other man's glowing eyes and, for a second, stopped breathing.

Willie reversed the knife in his hand and offered the handle to Delroy. "Take this," he said. "Mebbe you can saw through the strap."

THIRTY-THREE

Gilbert drove around Ocala, Florida for a couple of days to get the lay of the land. He had already determined his escape route using several maps, but he wanted to check for unknown hazards like road repairs and speed traps.

He decided not to stay at a motel. He slept in the back seat of his old Taurus and ate food from the drive-through windows of fast food restaurants. He didn't want anybody to remember him.

His current target lived in the Flamingo Harbor Retirement Village, a gated community with a guarded entrance and two unguarded exits. He parked across the street from one of the exits and waited for a delivery truck to leave. It wouldn't do to be seen by one of the residents, but a delivery driver wouldn't care.

Finally, a UPS truck pulled out, and Gilbert rocketed his car through before the gates closed. All the streets and houses looked the same to him, but he finally found the address he was looking for. He parked in the driveway and walked up to the front door.

THIRTY-FOUR

McKinney opened one eye and watched Carla pilot his car through the hot Tennessee evening. A trickle of sweat ran down his chest, and he rubbed at his shirt to blot it. He could hear Angelina, curled up on the back seat, snoring. Big Maceo was playing on the car stereo, and he tapped a finger on the armrest in time to "Chicago Breakdown." Carla looked at McKinney and turned down the volume. "Aren't you supposed to be napping?" she asked.

"I'm just worried about my grandmother. Angelina's got me thinking she might really be in some danger. I phoned her before we left. Turns out the gang she knew back in the thirties is the same gang this killer is asking about."

"You don't really think he'd track her down in Florida, do you?"

"I don't know, probably not. Just the same, maybe we should have flown."

"You're unemployed, remember? Airline tickets on short notice are expensive. Just relax."

"I'll try. It's no reflection on you, though. You're a good driver. When I was a kid we'd go on family vacations every summer, and my dad would never let my mother drive. He'd drive for twelve or fourteen hours straight, then pull in to a motel right after dozing at the wheel and almost killing us. That was usually about seven in the evening because he made us get up at dawn to beat the morning rush hour traffic."

"You know," Carla said, "driving straight through is just as stupid as getting up at dawn. We're all tired and a few hours won't hurt. Can't we stop for the night?"

McKinney looked out the window at the trees rushing past and the undulating hills in the distance. The setting sun had turned the shadows a deep purple. *She's right*, he thought, *we're both too tired to keep driving.*

"Sure. Sounds like a plan."

"What's the next big town?" Carla asked.

McKinney consulted the hand-held GPS unit he'd brought along. "We just went through Nashville. Murfreesboro is next."

"Okay, let's stop in Murfreesboro."

"Great. Civil War battlefield, the ghosts of three thousand dead soldiers, the perfect place to spend the night."

"How do you know that?"

"My dad was an amateur historian. It was his hobby. On our family vacations he would drag us from one historical site to the next, lecturing us about the battles and how each one helped to shape the current geography and politics of the country. The way people view history is pretty depressing. It's mostly a record of the violence and conflict created by one group of people trying to wrest land, or power, or natural resources, from another group of people."

"Just like on the evening news," she said. "Didn't your dad ever take you to see the world's largest ball of string, or to the Grand Canyon, or anything like that?"

McKinney rested his arm on the windowsill and his head on his arm so he could feel the night air on his face. The air smelled moist and mossy. "When I was Angelina's age I was crazy about rock and roll. I went through three copies of the Stones' *Out Of Our Heads* album because I played it so often. That summer, we went to New Orleans, and even though I was only seventeen, my dad took us to all these bars and nightclubs to listen to jazz and blues musicians. He had a whole series of lectures prepared about the historical roots of rock and roll and how famous rockers had taken licks from traditional jazz and blues. We ate delicious food I didn't even know existed, and learned about voodoo and pirates. Until that vacation, I didn't think my dad had any interest in who I was. It was great."

"Sounds like you miss him."

"Yeah. I'm just starting to realize how little I appreciated him. I tried to distance myself from him as a kid. When I was seventeen I bought my first car, and I made sure it had a manual transmission so he couldn't drive it. He had a bum left leg, broke it as a kid, and it didn't set right or something. All our family cars, when I was growing up, had automatic transmissions."

"Couldn't your mother have driven your car?"

"She could have," McKinney said, "but she wouldn't. The walking parts of our vacations were spent trying to keep up with Dad, while he limped along at breakneck speed. He'd only stop when he wanted to lecture us about some historic monument. It was like he was overcompensating for his imperfection. I think he lived most of his life that way."

"What do you mean?"

"Nothing he did was ever good enough. He applied that same standard to his family. He was smart enough not to compare us to other people—we weren't in competition with anyone—but, because he never set benchmarks, the goals he gave us were always unattainable. It was frustrating, but it was probably his pushing that got me through college." McKinney turned his head and stole a glance at Angelina. "I wish he were alive to see what a delightful person his granddaughter is. My mom misses him, too. They were crazy about each other. How about your parents?"

"Well, my mom's still around, too. She lives in Albuquerque. She moved there five years ago, after my dad died. He was killed in the same car crash that killed Ricky, my husband. They were both wonderful men. I miss them a lot. I've got a story about my dad that I like to remember, too."

"Let's hear it."

"Well, I blossomed kind of early when I was a girl."

"You mean you got boobs?"

"Yes, Sean, I got boobs. I got my training bra when I was ten. By the time I was in high school I had an entourage of boys hanging out at our house, competing for my attention. My dad was worried about it, but he knew he couldn't prevent me from seeing them, and talking to the boys wouldn't do any good, they were boys. Besides, his English wasn't very good. On my fourteenth birthday every present he gave me had a picture of a bumblebee on it. I got a sweater with a bee, a notebook with a bee, a stuffed animal shaped like a bee, everything bees. After the party he took me aside and told me about the bees. Not 'the birds and the bees' but about the way bees see things. Apparently, bees can see light in the ultraviolet spectrum as well as in the spectrum of light that we see."

"That's right," McKinney said. "On some flowers there are designs on the petals that only reflect ultraviolet light. Humans can't see the designs, only bees and a few other insects can. Hey, I'm impressed."

"Thanks. I guess the bees see the designs and are attracted to the flowers that have them. So, my dad said, 'Chachita—'"

"Wait. He called you Chachita?"

"Yeah, when I was little I reminded him of a Mexican actress called Chachita Muñoz. Anyway, he said, 'Chachita, you are like that flower. You have something special, but none of these boys can see it. They are like flies. They buzz around you all the time, but they only see your body. They can't see what makes you special. You need to be very careful, and look hard until you find a bee.'"

McKinney looked at her. "I see it. I've got the bumblebee eye. That's a nice story. Mind if I use it for Angelina?"

Angelina's sleepy voice floated up from the back seat. "If you do, I swear, I'll run away from home and join the circus."

THIRTY-FIVE

They carried the bundle up to the house. Delroy wanted to get off the lakeshore as quickly as possible, in case someone should see the glow from their lantern. They went into the living room and cleared a space on the floor to sit, kicking aside glass, plaster, and shell casings. The package was about the size of two loaves of bread, laid side by side, wrapped tight in brown oilcloth and dipped in wax on the ends. Willie used the butt of his knife to break off the wax, and Delroy tugged at the oilcloth until it split open and spilled paper-wrapped packets of money onto the floor between them. Willie started to let out a whoop, but Delroy shushed him.

"Let's not broadcast it, Willie. The sooner we divide this up and get out of here, the better I'll like it."

"That's a fact."

The paper wrappers on the money were printed with the legend, Banco de Cuba. Delroy had heard Freddie and Karpis discussing ways to unload money they couldn't spend. That's why Freddie kept a hideout in Florida. The ransom money from the kidnapping had been sold in Cuba for unmarked bills. The FBI would have a list of the serial numbers on the ransom, but not on this money. It was clean.

They counted out thirty-seven packets with five hundred dollars in each, and one packet that had been opened, for a total of eighteen thousand, six hundred and forty-three dollars. Delroy divided the bundles into two stacks, nine thousand three hundred and twenty-one dollars for each man. He gave Willie the extra dollar. "Something to remember me by," he said.

Willie tore the dollar and handed half back to Delroy. "Fifty, fifty, mister. Just like you said."

The men took off their shirts and each wrapped up their share of the money to carry home. Delroy blew out the candle and Willie followed him out into the moonlight. Delroy wedged his bundle under the front seat of the Model A and turned back to Willie. "Give you a lift?" he asked.

"Thank yuh. But I reckon I'll walk back the way I come."

Delroy held out his hand one last time. "It's been a real pleasure. You take care, now."

Willie pumped Delroy's hand again. "Youse the most honest white man I ever met."

Delroy thought about the robberies he'd done with Freddie and the people who'd been killed or injured. "Willie, I wish that was true."

It was after midnight when Delroy got back to the Gulf Breeze, but Lucille was still awake, and anxious. He made her sit on the bed while he secured the room. Despite the heat, he closed all the windows and drew the shades. He ignored her pleas to tell her what he'd found and wedged a chair under the doorknob.

Finally, he unfurled his damp shirt and let the packets of money tumble out onto the bed in front of her. Lucille stared at the pile of green but didn't touch it. Delroy sat cross-legged on the bed in front of her. He split open a packet and fanned the bills under her nose. "Go ahead," he said. "It's real." He picked up her hand and started stacking bills on her palm. "It's our money, honey, and we are going to have us a time!" He smacked the bottom of her hand, sending the pile of bills up in the air. They fluttered down around them on the bed. He picked up a ten-dollar bill, licked it, and stuck it to his forehead. "First thing, we'll move to a nicer place, maybe on the north side, and we'll get a car, and you'll have all the pretty dresses you want. And I'm gonna get me one of them silk hats, like the rich men wear when they take their wives downtown on Saturday night."

"How much is it?" Lucille asked.

Delroy grabbed both her hands and started bouncing on the bed. The money bounced in between them. "More than nine thousand dollars. Nine thousand...three hundred...twenty-one...dollars!"

"We can spend the three hundred and twenty-one dollars," she said. "The rest is for the baby."

"What?" Delroy stopped bouncing. "What are you talking about? That's nine thousand dollars!"

Lucille's face hardened, and she looked Delroy in the eyes. "This baby is going to school. He's going to be the healthiest, happiest baby there ever was, and he's going to grow up and get an education, and that money is going to make sure he doesn't have to try and scrape a living out of Rockcastle County clay. That money ain't even ours. It rightly belongs to some man those damn Barkers kidnapped. Do you think for one minute I'd keep it if I didn't have this baby to worry about?" She stopped talking and tried to catch her breath while she waited for an answer. Delroy saw the determined look on her face and was overcome with admiration for the grit of this little country woman. He smiled and pulled her closer until they were nose to nose.

"Now, Missus McKinney," he said. "Why didn't I think of that?"

THIRTY-SIX

Is this iced tea already sweetened?" Gilbert asked. He took a green plastic pitcher and a package of sliced, yellow cheese out of the refrigerator, closing the door with his hip.

Lucille McKinney sat at the kitchen table shaking her head. Her hands were folded in front of her and she rested them on the lustrous white tabletop. She was bound at the wrists with nylon cable ties. "You should be ashamed. I'm going to be ninety-five years old, day after tomorrow." She lifted her hands to her bruised chin. "Didn't your mama raise you any better than to hit an old lady?"

"Well, see now, that may be the problem, granny. My mother didn't raise me." He opened one of the lilac-colored cabinets over the sink. "Where do you keep your sugar?"

"Sugar bowl's on the counter, by the toaster."

Gilbert poured two glasses of tea and carried them to the table. He flipped a chair around backwards and straddled it, so he sat facing Lucille. "You having a birthday party?"

"My grandson—" Lucille said, then quickly closed her mouth, tight.

Gilbert saw the color drain out of her lips and the wrinkles at the corners of her eyes deepen. "Don't worry," he said. "You and me are going to get to know one another over the next couple of days. We won't have any secrets from each other by your birthday." He looked around the kitchen at the spotless counter and appliances, all gleaming white. The overhead light was off and the shade was drawn across the sliding glass door leading to the back yard. It was a sunny afternoon outside but only a feeble light penetrated to the kitchen. The dimness made the perfectly cleaned furnishings seem even brighter. "This is, without a doubt, the cleanest kitchen I've ever seen." He unwrapped a slice of cheese and tossed it on the table. It landed with a wet smack. Gilbert peeled it up and ate it. "You could probably eat off the floor in here, too." He unwrapped another slice of cheese, wadded it into a ball, and threw it at Lucille. It hit her in the neck and rolled off, onto the floor. She shivered. "I tell you what," he said. "I'll go first. I'll tell you one of my secrets, then you tell me one of yours. Okay, here goes. I've killed women in kitchens just like this, maybe not as clean, but kitchens all the same. The women were about your age, too." He pulled the little Beretta out of his pocket and placed it on the table next to his glass. "I shot them with this gun."

"I told you—" she started.

Gilbert raised his hand. "Ah, ah. Not yet." He reached out and spun the gun on the table, as if he were playing a game of spin the bottle. The gun came to a stop pointing off to the side. He turned it to point at Lucille. "Cheating, I know, but what're you gonna do? Okay, your turn. Tell me everything you know about Freddie Barker and Alvin Karpis and their hidden gold coins. I've followed this chain of old farts from Chicago to Florida, and you, granny, are the last link. We're going to stay here until I'm satisfied that you've told me everything and, if your grandson shows up before we're through—" He picked up the gun and sighted down the short barrel. "Kapow!"

THIRTY-SEVEN

They arrived at the Flamingo Harbor Retirement Village with sunburned arms and sweat soaked shirts. Ocala was landlocked, a fact McKinney couldn't resist pointing out. "They call this place Flamingo Harbor, but there's obviously no harbor, and I'll bet you five bucks we never see a flamingo. They probably named it in honor of the birds that were killed or displaced by the developers."

"I'll be sure to tell Great-grandma that you noticed, Dad. I'm sure she'll appreciate your sciency powers of observation."

"Sciency, eh? I'll be glad when school starts again."

Angelina crossed her eyes and stuck her tongue in her cheek. "I done inherited my speechifyin' skills from you, Paw."

The guard at the gate had them on a list of expected visitors, and he gave McKinney a map of the community and showed him how to find his way. There was a car in the driveway, so they parked in front of the house and waded through the stifling, afternoon heat to the front door. The curtains were drawn, and no one answered the doorbell.

"This is the right house," Carla said. "Her name's on the mailbox."

"Maybe she keeps a key under the mat," McKinney said. He lifted the plastic doormat and knelt down. "Look at this."

"What?" Carla asked. "A cockroach?"

"Nope." McKinney picked up a small, golden beetle. "This is a tortoise beetle. Probably the same species that inspired Poe's story, *The Gold Bug*." He let it crawl off his hand, onto a bush next to the small porch. "Like a lot of southerners, they enjoy sweet potatoes. No key, though."

Angelina cupped her hands around her eyes and tried to peer in through the front window. "It's three o'clock in the afternoon. Why are her curtains closed?"

"Maybe she's visiting a neighbor," McKinney said. "I'll go around the back and have a look." He walked along the side of the house and stepped over a low fence into the backyard. Beyond a patio covered with potted plants and lawn furniture was a sliding glass door. The curtains in front of it were closed as well. McKinney knocked for a minute, then put his ear up against the glass. He thought he heard something, but he couldn't be certain if it came from inside the house or was ambient neighborhood noise. He looked through the glass at the base of the door, expecting to see the wooden bar that people sometimes use to prevent sliding doors from opening, but there wasn't one. Then he noticed the door itself. There were scratch marks around the latch, and the aluminum frame was bent back. Stress cracks in the glass radiated out from the handle. Someone had popped the lock.

McKinney shivered a little. He pulled his cell phone from his pocket, keyed in 911 and rested his thumb on the 'send' button. Using the back of his hand, he slid the door open and stepped through the curtains, from the afternoon sun into a dark kitchen. He was startled to see his grandmother lying on the floor facing him. There was something across her mouth, and her eyes were big and white in the gloom. She made a muffled noise, and then, as his eyes adjusted, he saw a man standing behind her. The man was pointing something at him. Before he could move, McKinney felt a sharp pain in his head and fell down. He was aware of the cool tile against his cheek and a nasty, sulfur smell stinging his nose. Then, awareness left him.

When he opened his eyes he still couldn't see. He was lying face down on the floor of a dark bedroom. He tried to turn his head, but it hurt too much. He was aware that his hands were fastened behind his back, but he didn't know why. He knew he was in Florida, at his grandmother's house, but he couldn't think of anything that would explain being tied up or the pain in his head, so he closed his eyes and went back to sleep.

The next time McKinney opened his eyes he willed them to stay open. He knew that something was wrong. A hazy light illuminating a slice of carpet told him where the door was. Beyond it, he could hear voices and what sounded like crying. Angelina? With an effort, he rolled onto his side and pushed his hands, joined at the wrists, down past his hips. He had to slip his shoes off to get his feet through, but the flexibility gained from years of tai chi practice paid off. Soon his hands were in front of him and he could see the linked nylon cable ties that bound him. He pushed himself forward until he lay next to the open gap in the door. The air conditioning was off, and the combination of heat and effort drenched him in sweat. Now he could make out the voices. He recognized his grandmother's lilting drawl.

"Son, you may as well wish in one hand and spit in the other and see which one fills up first. I've told you a dozen times, I don't know about any gold coins."

There was a smack, and the crying got louder. His grandmother raised her voice.

"What in the hell did you hit *her* for? She's just a

youngster."

McKinney began to panic. Someone was hitting his little girl. He covered his mouth with his hands in an attempt to muffle his loud breathing and struggled to get his fear under control.

A voice he hadn't heard before, a man's voice, answered. "We've been at this for almost two days now, granny, and I'm just about out of patience. From now on, every time I get an answer I don't like I'm going to beat one of these two and let you watch. I killed an old guy's sweet little dogs to get him to talk, and I won't hesitate to kill this 'youngster' if I think you're not being straight with me."

McKinney pushed himself up to his knees and, when he did, blood ran across his forehead and down his face. It tasted salty. *If my blood's still flowing freely,* he thought, *I can't have been out long.* The carpet where his head had rested was stained dark. He crawled over to the bed, used the pillow to wipe the blood out of his eye, and ran his hands across his head until he found the wound. Despite the throbbing pain, the site of the wound was numb. He couldn't feel his fingers touching his head, but when he brought them away they were shiny with blood. He let out a little moan and quickly stifled it. Was he dying? He looked desperately around the room. He had to call the police, but even in the dark he could see there was no phone. He patted his empty pants pocket. His cell phone was gone. Pulling the pillow off the bed, he pressed it against his wound and crawled back to the door. He heard Carla speaking.

"Listen, mister, I've got several thousand dollars in the bank. Take me to an ATM and I'll show you. You can have every cent I've got if you let us go."

"Do you have four million dollars?" Gilbert asked.

Carla's voice quavered. "I've got at least five thousand."

"Four million is the figure we're looking for here, lady. Unless you can get me four million dollars I suggest you shut the fuck up."

"Boy," McKinney's grandmother said, "you don't have the sense God gave a grasshopper. Why would gold coins still be setting around after seventy years? Just because they were never reported found doesn't mean anything. After the law killed Freddie and his mother they probably split it up between them and promised not to tell anyone. That money's long gone."

"I think you're lying," Gilbert said. His voice rose. "It's too big a coincidence, you living down here just a few miles from Lake Weir."

"This is where my husband and I used to come for vacation. He worked for the Greyhound bus, and we could go anywhere we wanted. At first we thought it was funny to be so close to where the Barkers got killed, but we liked it here, so we kept coming back."

McKinney heard another smack, followed by Angelina's frightened sobbing. Tears mixed with the blood that was running down his face. He looked frantically around the room for something to use as a weapon.

"Come on now," his grandmother said, "even if I had the money, there wouldn't be anything left of it. Do you know how much assisted living costs? You have to sign away everything you own before they let you move in. The crooks that run this place are worse than Freddie and Doc ever were."

The words 'assisted living' made McKinney stop and think. He looked around the room again. If this was Grandma Lucy's bedroom there had to be a call button to contact the medical staff in case of an emergency. On the floor, by the head of the bed, he saw a box connected to the wall by a short cable. He must have pulled it off the bed with the pillow. He crawled over to it and jabbed the button repeatedly, glaring at the little speaker on the box. There was no answer. He crawled back to the door. If he went out there, the man would kill him. If he didn't go, the bastard would kill his daughter.

"Well, I guess you're right, granny," Gilbert said. "The gold's gone, and I've got no more use for any of you. Who should I kill first, the youngster?"

McKinney steadied himself against the wall and pushed up to his feet. "Well, Catherine," he whispered, "let's go get our girl." He waited for the dizziness to pass, then quietly opened the door and moved down the hall. Thankfully, the man was facing away from him. The three women were lined up on a couch, hands in their laps, with their wrists bound in front of them. McKinney inched out toward the man. A metallic voice from the bedroom drawled, "Are you all right, ma'am? What do you need?" and Gilbert spun toward McKinney.

McKinney shouted as he rushed him. He tried to yell, "You can't have her!" but all that came out was "Yooouuuuu!" Gilbert brought the little Beretta up from his side and fired. McKinney never felt the bullet enter his chest. He lowered his center of gravity, stepped his front foot between Gilbert's legs and, leading with his *dan tian*, shifted his weight, slamming his shoulder into Gilbert's chest. Gilbert flew backwards and bounced off the wall. He let go of the gun to catch himself as he fell forward, and it skittered away from him, stopping in front of the couch. Lucille McKinney struggled to reach it with her bound hands. She picked up the gun and, as Gilbert got up from the floor, emptied the clip into his stomach. He teetered on the balls of his feet, almost toppling forward, and then, his eyes wide and his arms flailing, staggered back and forth from one foot to the other. McKinney thought it looked like he was dancing an abbreviated tarantella, the tarantula dance.

Finally, Gilbert fell back down to lie, twitching, at Lucille's feet. McKinney sat down, hard, on the floor. He saw Angelina staring at him with fright-filled eyes. He wanted to reassure her but found it difficult to speak, so he held up his bound hands, smiled and waved. He had never been so happy. Then the blackness took him again.

EPILOGUE

The members of the Cubbies Garden Club were all wearing sweaters under their smocks while they picked the last of the beans and squash. The air was crisp and damp. Mrs. Vladic had on her official Cubs hat and, despite another losing season for her beloved team, was hopeful for next year. "They were just breaking in the new pitching staff this year," she explained. She said the same thing after every season. She held up a small pumpkin. "Hey, McKinney, you want this? You could carve a little jack-o-lantern while you're recuperating."

McKinney was sitting in a lawn chair, drinking hot tea. Carla and Angelina had made him wear a sweater, a jacket, and a Cubs hat. A little strip of Steritape stuck out from under the brim. The tea he drank was Vishal's pungent, homemade chai.

"Sure. Thanks, Mrs. V." He turned back to Vishal, who was sitting next to the vegetable-covered patio table. "So, there was plenty of physical evidence, after all. They matched Anglin's shoe to the shoeprints left at Arnold Drenon and Florence Burdett's houses, his blood to a smear that was on a glass chip from Florence Burdett's, and some scratches on the windowsill of a St. Paul nursing home to a screwdriver in his luggage. He had Gertrude Hoskins's diary in his suitcase, and they found a mess of dog hair on one of his shirts. It was lucky for Phillips that Anglin survived, though. He admitted that he'd worked alone."

"So, no one has ever found the missing gold coins?" Vishal asked.

"I doubt there ever were any gold coins. That was probably just a story Karpis made up to impress the other inmates at Alcatraz. As it turns out, my grandparents found some of the gang's money—in bills—way back in the 1930s. They just conveniently forgot to mention it to anyone for over seventy years."

"That is quite a story. So, your grandmother actually has all that money?"

"No. She said there was only about nine thousand dollars. They spent the last of it long before Gilbert Anglin was even born. He was a fool."

"Maybe that money helped them raise your father, who was then able to raise you, so you could go to Florida and save your grandmother's life."

"Karma?" McKinney asked.

Vishal grinned. Carla and Angelina plopped bags of zucchinis and eggplants on the table and came over to where McKinney sat. Carla lifted the brim of his hat and kissed him on the head.

"That's not very sanitary," he said. "You don't want me to get an infection do you?"

She kissed him on the mouth. "Don't you ever stop talking?"

"Only for kissing and eating," he said. "I've had the kissing, now when do we eat? You wrapped me up like a mummy and stuck me in this chair without any provisions. I'm starving."

"Maybe next year you'd like to help with the gardening as well as the eating."

"I would." He realized that he meant it, and this surprised him. He had never tended a garden before.

"Don't go away," Carla said. "I'll be right back." She ran up the back steps to her apartment and returned carrying a large package wrapped in brown paper and tied with string. She plopped it on McKinney's lap and handed him a pair of scissors. "From me to you," she said. McKinney hefted the heavy package, then cut the string. The brown paper peeled away to reveal Carla's statue of the little girl playing in the rain. Suddenly he felt like crying. He managed to croak out a, "Thank you."

Angelina took the statue out of his hands and pulled him to his feet. "It's getting cold. You should go in, Dad. We've just got to clean up down here, and then we'll start dinner." She gave him a little shove in the direction of the stairs.

"Hey, McKinney!" A voice from behind him made McKinney stop and look around. A blonde woman in a business suit was coaxing a young man across the lawn.

"Nina," he said, "how are you?" He stuck out his hand.

The lawyer pulled him into a hug and gave him a peck on the cheek. She caught the annoyed look on Carla's face and stepped back. "Look at you," she said. "You look pretty frisky for someone they pulled two bullets out of. Have you started back to work yet?"

McKinney shook his head. "Officially, I'm still fired, but the union's arranged a hearing for next week. We'll see."

"I'll keep my fingers crossed," she said, then gestured toward the young man beside her. "This is John Phillips. He wanted to meet you."

McKinney looked at Phillips. He was wearing the same ill-fitting suit he'd worn at the courthouse. "Hello, John," McKinney said. "Nice to meet you."

Phillips looked nervous. He fixed his eyes on a bag of pole beans at McKinney's feet.

"I just wanted to thank you, Mr. McKinney. You saved my life. Prison was awful. I never would have made it in that place."

"Well, I'm glad I could help," McKinney said. He motioned toward Nina Anderson. "You had a good lawyer, too."

Phillips finally looked up, and when he did, McKinney held out his hand. Phillips shook it.

"Do you like Halloween, John?" McKinney asked. Phillips nodded his head, and McKinney walked over to the patio table. He handed Phillips the little pumpkin and gestured to the members of the Cubbies Garden Club, who had all stopped their harvesting to listen to the conversation. "My friends here grew this pumpkin in their garden, and I'd like you to have it. It would make a nice jack-o-lantern, don't you think?"

Phillips nodded and took the pumpkin. He carried it with both hands as his lawyer led him out the gate and back to her car. McKinney smiled as he watched them go.

HISTORICAL NOTE

The Barker/Karpis gang was responsible for numerous payroll and bank robberies in the Midwestern United States during the 1930s. They have also been credited with two kidnappings, those of Minneapolis banker Edward Bremer, Jr. and William Hamm, Jr., heir to the Hamm's beer fortune. The two kidnappings netted them a total of $300,000.

The core of the gang consisted of Alvin "Creepy" Karpis, Kate "Ma" Barker, and her two sons, Arthur (Doc) and Freddie. Ma had two other sons—Lloyd, who was serving a twenty-five-year sentence in Leavenworth, and Herman, who committed suicide in 1927. In addition to Karpis and the Barkers, the gang had a floating roster of members that changed depending on the job and whoever happened to be out of prison.

The gang kept safe houses in Chicago and St. Paul, Minnesota. St. Paul in the 1930s was a haven for criminals. It was well known that if a gangster had the cash he could lay low there in comfort. It was in St. Paul that the Barkers met Jack Peifer, owner of the Hollyhocks Club, who helped them plan the Hamm kidnapping. While in Chicago, the gang hired Dr. Joseph Moran to perform plastic surgery on several of the boys and to wipe out their fingerprints. By all accounts, he botched the operations and was murdered to keep him from talking.

Doc Barker was arrested in 1934 and sentenced to life in Alcatraz where he was killed trying to escape. Freddie and Ma Barker died in January 1935, in a shootout with FBI agents at a secluded house on Lake Weir in central Florida.

Not long after that Alvin Karpis and another gang member,

Harry Campbell, were almost caught in Atlantic City. They escaped, leaving behind their girlfriends to be picked up by the police. Over a year later the FBI arrested Alvin Karpis at a rooming house in New Orleans. J. Edgar Hoover stated that he personally took part in the famous capture but, in his autobiography, *The Alvin Karpis Story*, Karpis claimed that Hoover hid around the corner of a building and only came out when he got the "all clear" from his agents.

Another discrepancy between the official FBI story of the time and Karpis's version of events is the latter's assertion that Ma Barker "didn't have the brains or know-how to direct us on a robbery." The story, put forth by Hoover and popularized in dozens of true crime magazines, comic books, and movies such as *Ma Barker's Killer Brood* and *Bloody Mama*, was that Ma Barker was a criminal mastermind who trained her sons to rob and kill, and planned their jobs. Karpis's take on Ma was different. She was, he said, just Doc and Freddie's mother, and whenever the gang needed to plan a job they sent her to the movies. According to Karpis, "Ma saw a lot of movies."

Tim Chapman is a former forensic scientist for the Chicago police department who currently teaches writing and tai chi chuan. He holds a Master's degree in Creative Writing from Northwestern University. His short fiction has been published in The Southeast Review, the Chicago Reader, Alfred Hitchcock's Mystery Magazine, Chicago Tribune's Printers Row Journal, and the anthology, *The Rich and the Dead*. His first novel, *A Trace of Gold* (originally published as *Bright and Yellow, Hard and Cold),* was a finalist in Shelf Unbound's 2013 Best Indie Book competition. His short stories have been collected under the title, *Kiddieland and other misfortunes*. In his spare time he paints pretty pictures and makes an annoying noise with his saxophone that he claims is music. He lives in Chicago with his lovely and patient wife, Ellen, and Mia, the squirrel-chasingest dog in town.

Praise for *Kiddieland and other misfortunes*

Chapman's powerful writing shines. His deep and touching stories resonate with real emotion. The heartbreaking "What We Do For Love" and "A Flash of Lightning," the timeless revenge of "Dirty Water," the tenderness of "The Gentile Grift" — and of course, the gut-wrenching climax of the title story "Kiddieland" — add up to a volume of stories that are so good you'll want to read them all in a single sitting. But don't! Savor the complex nuances of each story individually."
—J. Michael Major, author of *One Man's Castle*

"Tim Chapman is a writer's writer. His prose, his plots, and characters are some of the best you'll ever see. This guy can WRITE!"
—Libby Fischer Hellmann, author of *Nobody's Child* and *Set the Night on Fire*

"Tim Chapman is equally adept writing in the spheres of sci-fi, horror, mystery, personal relationships, and childhood memories. A rich mixture of stories indeed!"
—Robert Goldsborough, author of *Archie in the Crosshairs, a Nero Wolfe mystery*

"A riveting collection of accidental heroes, the lonely and the lost, unexpected cruelties and unlooked-for redemptions… Tim Chapman's tales in Kiddieland and other misfortunes draw you in from the first page and don't let you go."
—D. M. Pirrone, author of *Shall We Not Revenge* and *No Less In Blood*